This Book e n i t, Maria

It Comes

'Belonging to the realm of folk tales, a rich seam of earthly delights runs through the book; the seductive smell of simmering food, the mellowing effect of wine...This tale of redemption celebrates the triumph of love and forgiveness over resentment and intransigence, told with conviction, charm, and flashes of humour in a highly individualistic style.'
Rosa Stepanova, *Shetland Daily News*

'Such a brilliant read I couldn't bear to put it down, each page a delight for the senses (while) describing the human frailties that can overwhelm and crush our relationships...showing that what is broken can be fixed and made even better and stronger than before.'
Amazon.co.uk

'This poetic journey reminds us to be kind to others, appreciate each day and see the beauty around us...(with) many twists and turns and a surprise waiting for us at each stage. An uplifting and easy read.'
Simon Heather, author of *The Healing Power of Sound*

Challenging, compelling, and uplifting. A triumph of the human spirit over adversity.
Amazon.com

'A bold uncompromising debut, this very original novel reads quickly but it is not a book (you'd) want to rush or skip through and certainly leaves the reader wanting more...one can't help wondering 'What happens next?' Could there be a sequel to this excellent novel?'
Laura Friedlander, *The Shetland Times*

ABOUT THE AUTHOR

Joy Perino was born in London, worked as a film and
television director for many years, and now lives in Shetland
with her husband and two dogs.

IT COMES

A route map for fanatics, bigots,
and domestic oppressors
gone astray

JOY PERINO

SALOSCHIN PUBLISHING
SHETLAND

SALOSCHIN PUBLISHING

Skelberry
Vidlin
Shetland ZE2 9QD

www.saloschin.co.uk

First published by Saloschin Publishing 2010

2

Copyright ©Joy Perino 2010

All rights reserved

The moral right of the author has been asserted

A CIP catalogue record for this book
is available from the British Library

This book is sold subject to the condition that it shall not,
by way of trade or otherwise, be lent, re-sold, hired out or otherwise
circulated without the publisher's prior consent
in any form of binding or cover other than that in which it
is published and without a similar condition including this
condition being imposed on the subsequent purchaser

ISBN 978-1-907834-00-4

For Chris, always

1

It comes. It comes by train, with the man who carries all life with him like a sack, a burden of weights. He lifts it down from the baggage rail and it drops heavily onto the seat then the floor and smashes open, spilling all content, all life and woes over the floor of the carriage. Things roll under seats and are found by children clambering over each other to get at the elusive and shiny treasures skittering past them on their way, rolling rolling rolling to who knows where.

All are vital and alive to the sight of the woes rolling past them, and look and sigh with sadness at the poor old man who hates them but cannot let them go and is on his hands and knees, crawling, scampering like a dog, trying to gather his misery back to him before it escapes and is lost for good. What would he be without it, them, his lost and loosed treasures?

Life has been delineated by his woes, the very life-blood of him. One by one they have burnt small holes in his soul as they carve their way up, from his feet to his head, searing their way through his bones and skeleton and veins and organs as they make their way out to break free through his head, his eyes, and ears and nose and mouth, orifices for release that allow the woes to vent and fight and yell their sudden freedom.

Roar. He roars his rage and fury, the last tiny woe breaking free through his throat, chakra of truth and communion, and it flies into the air in blue light and dances free and expansive and full of the light of spring, the spring outside the train window that he doesn't see, doesn't ever see because his sack is too heavy to allow him to raise his head and smell the clover and see the milk and honey before him. His misery is too important to him to allow views of golden light and dancing flowers to interrupt the view of gloom and doom and desperate darkness that he has become accustomed to. His view. His easy and easily recognised landscape of barren waste and wasted years, of hope dashed and thrashed against rocks of misery and despair.

He likes his view now. He wants no change at his age, advanced age he thinks, no idea just how old he really is – thinks only in human terms when in reality he is much much older than he knows now, in this incarnation of doom and sadness and clung-to despair.

He waits as children and women gather up the symbols of his past. Magnets that draw him ever over and over to assess and reassess all that has gone and been and been done to him and by him and for him. He sees his life in a flash of painful clarity and sees the dark and the evil he has perpetrated and the light shows him he is the burden, has built his house of woes and imprisoned those he loved within its invisible walls of darkness.

They clamoured to be set free and he held ever tighter, knowing they saw light and dancing flowers, could smell the honey bees and the clover and the gifts waiting to be poured down on them from above, from God's bounty that is there for all if they just choose to share it.

He could not bear to see them happy away from him, though he knew he was the cause of their misery, yet he could not change, so he told himself, we are what we are, God made us as we are and so we stay, unmoving, unchanging, because change is blasphemy.

Could not see what all could see, that change is life, growth, the seasons of body and soul, and change and stasis have a place in the interchange of life and love and being and doing that is the blood of creation. His head would not lift up to see that view. "Too heavy" he said.

Not the view for him. A view for fools who believe in fairies and rainbows and pots of gold. "A fool is blind to the truth" he said, knowing in his heart the fool was him, but not allowing that thought to break free and travel the channels and paths and highways of his blood and bones and skeleton and creep slowly to his mind. He wanted none of that knowledge because then what? How many wasted years of keeping hold and working hard and being in misery inside and out, what would that have been for? Does not punishment and endurance make a soul fit for God?

Would all the fools who took life easy and danced and rained gold on shop keepers and women and dance and song, would they be fit for God? "What's the point then" he'd think? But then he'd see them die happy, beatific smiles on their stupid idle faces, and wonder if he got it wrong, if they got it right, and a happy life is a good life.

Had he denied himself all these years, denied them, his wife and daughters in their grey rags at their prime, dull as ditchwater when they should be shining like stars under a firmament made for and of blessings? Had he given them purgatory for nothing? Had they missed their chance at heaven because he got it wrong? Made the wrong choice early on and lived a lifetime based on a bad idea, an idea of wasted opportunity for life to shower it's bounty on him?

Too hard to take. Can't take it. Won't. Denial is good. Breathe. Sigh. Yes.

And so life rolled on, easy for some, hard for him and his beleaguered family, until the sight of the daisies flowering for another spring, another season of disenchantment and closing the door on light and laughter grew too much and they left him, every one of them, gone to finally breathe in life as it was and is meant to be. And he is alone now with his bag of woes rolling about the carriage floor, handled by curious onlookers as they hand them back, uncertain about the feel of them, slightly distasteful and eager and happy to have them taken out of their hands once more. "Sticky and odd and unnecessarily strange," they think.

Women smile politely then take their children by the hand and hold tight in case the strange old man somehow infects them with his weirdness and the odd grey gloom that seems settled around him like a cloud of midges and flies, buzzing buzzing buzzing but going nowhere because they have found their home.

* * *

He gets off the train and steps into a different world – a place of flowers on the platform, strangers smiling and welcoming him, even a little band playing as if saluting his arrival.

He has come searching for them, tired of being alone in his solitude – he preferred the solitude enmasse, all pining and gazing longingly out at the abundance of others and wallowing in the lack of their own.

Now he sees they have found their place of abundance and it has light and colour and smells that are familiar and unfamiliar to him – sweet scents of honeysuckle and lavender and fresh washing and coffee on a stove and fresh bread and bacon and cakes on a windowsill.

Life is in full flow here in this new place they have chosen as home. Not the stalled greyness and sour scent of old home, his home still, where he is hoping to return and take them with him, but he sees that will not happen. They will not leave this new paradise of honey and cats purring round his ankles. They are here to stay and he knows it, and his heart understands it but again, that blockage, his blood and bones and skeleton won't let the thought make the journey up to his mind and mouth and allow him to speak it to himself, to acknowledge a truth spread clearly before him, a truth he is invited to share if only he can leave the rags of his old life behind, step out of them and allow a new skin to emerge to cover and bathe him clean, purify the old and renew all, all cells, all blood and bones and skeleton to bring on new life, new abundance, new will to live and be and love and find life renewed, ever renewing, ever abundant, raining down like a summer

thunderstorm, deluging and flash flooding till all
the old is washed away leaving green – spring.

"Let the prayers begin." Ding. "We are here, gathered today, to sing the praises of and to the Lord, are we not?"

"Yes" responds the crowd.

"Gather round, hear this story. Tell it to the children and the children's children, of a man and a family, all grown now, but once as you, little children, and their choices made them into who they were and are now. Some choices were good, some bad, like us all. They led them this way and that, but ultimately all leads to God. He helps us, and tries to help us, but sometimes we choose not to let him, then our choices become dark and diseased and we find ourselves outside the flow of universal love. Then again we can choose to step back into that flow at any time, if we choose to. You see? Choices. All along the way, choices, made by us, only us, ourselves, inside to translate outside. Do you understand children?"

All the children nod their heads and a few shouts of "Yes" are heard from the back – a vocal child who will grow to be a singer and sing chants from the holy lands to all as popular songs. The music will heal and transform all who hear it, and his journey begins here, today, now, with a childish desire to do as he's told and make a choice, a good choice, to stay in the flow of God. He chooses music because he loves to sing and yell, and the noise and volume will be trained and tuned over time to make beautiful sounds that do not grate on the ear as he does now. All because the Priest said "make a good choice".

He obeys. Who else?

A child chooses to feed its dog nicer morsels, unbeknownst to its mother who keeps the animal chained outside to deter thieves. She chooses to trust in God to keep the thieves in the flow and away from her house, and at that same moment plans a little bed to be made and brought inside to house their little pet. The dog, at home, senses this imminent change in the air and sets up his own song of praise and "Yes" to the heavens as he is about to step into the flow of abundance.

All leave lighter of heart and step, on to their tables and Sunday lunch and then an afternoon nap. Blessed day, blessed people, blessed flow all around them, all willingly and happily choosing to step into and remain inside it. Enfolded, cared for, loved, beloved. "My beloved" says the Lord to each and every one of them.

* * *

Peace reigns in this little place, and pots bubble on stoves and bottles of wine pop their corks as all settle into this warm fug of aroma of stew and roast and wine. A heady mix.

All but one. Pondering whether to stay or go. He has been here a while now. The train left without him long ago – he made a choice to stay – but he can't follow that choice through now. He watches the Station Master's wife cook her brisket amidst the green and abundant explosion of her kitchen, vegetables chopped and piled, tomatoes glistening in a bowl waiting to become salad, fennel tops feathery and saluting the air and filling it with their aniseed scent.

The Station Master helps his wife and pours them a glass of wine to help things along. Watching from a bench on the platform, the old man realises he never poured his wife a glass of wine. Never drank one himself. Yet somewhere in this place maybe that is what she is doing now. Maybe she and his, their, four girls are all sitting around a bright kitchen table, lit by the inevitable sun that pours down on this place. Sharing a glass of wine, or maybe even a sherry, risking all damnation and penance for the glow and pleasure of a sip of Andalusian fire – a gentle, rosy fire that he imagines gliding down their throats like molten gold. He'd like a sherry.

He'd like a sherry. A thought that has never before entered into the bleak and barren cavern of his mind. The grey and abandoned saloon of his brain rustles and hisses as the thick, deep cobwebs flutter in the unheard of breeze. Somewhere a door has opened; somehow, something or someone has remembered this place exists and has decided it's worth a visit. The cobwebs tilt and play in the growing air disturbance, and the dust shifts in anticipation. Who is coming?

A sherry. That's all. So much to ask? After a lifetime of denial, he'd like a sherry to toast his new arrival, even though it is much resented, and yet instead of raising a glass to welcome him, all these stupid idle peasants raise their glasses to each other and ignore him, him, sitting alone on a station bench long after the train has gone, his bag of woes now back at his side, fully restocked.

He watches the happy couple sip their wine and stir the brisket and chop the tomatoes and fennel so their scent fills the air and reaches his nose.

He's hungry too. And is that fresh bread he can smell? Crusty, broken off, dipped in the rich salady juices and raised dripping and crumbly to his mouth.

Too much. All these senseless and greedy people. He's going home. But when's the next train?

He marches, more a belligerent shuffle in reality, over the tracks and up to the open window of the Station Master's kitchen and knocks his stick against the open frame.

They start, then turn to see this grey-faced stranger scowling in at them and their food and wine. His glowering breaks a little as he scans their repast, but snaps back as he returns his attention to their idleness and greed and his need to get out of here and back to his familiar territory of bleak and barren and dusty gloom.

"When's the next train?" he barks.

"Tomorrow" comes the inevitable reply – couldn't be today could it? Have to be another day so he is forced to watch their shameless indulgence and even be forced to ask, beg, to be included in it since he has nowhere to go to sleep. The indignity. The shame. The pollution of his rigid soul, made hard and dark for God through his years of penance. All to be compromised by having to spend the night in this place of wanton indulgence.

"You'll have to stay" says the Station Master's wife, as if that wasn't obvious enough to him.

"Do you have somewhere? Do you know people here?" Ah. The question. The big question which he has been trying to ignore, put to the back of his mind, forget. Forget the reason he came here at all. Does he know them? His wife and children? He thinks "No, I never knew them, they lied to me and deceived me, if this place was in their hearts the whole time. I never knew them."

"No" he replies "I know nobody here. I got off at the wrong stop."

"Have a glass of wine and we'll sort you out" says the Station Master, and his hand shoots out through the open window, holding out a glass of ruby wine, slopping a little up the sides and running in a glistening tear of red down the side, to hang and sway on the bottom rim like an upside down poppy.

The old man watches the drip as it detaches and falls and lands on his shoe. Instantly the dust from the journey is gone and the colour of the old and cracked leather shows through, aged but beautiful still as the red of the wine sinks in and nourishes and colours it.

He looks at the proffered refreshment but his hand won't reach out to it. He can smell it though, God's grape, shining there for him now, offering itself for his refreshing and renewing. Does he choose to take it? Will he allow temptation in? Will he heck.

He turns from the Station Master's window and, rage boiling up inside him at how the devil briefly was allowed to tempt him, marches down the platform and out of the station.

Into a quiet, slightly dusty, hot town, basking in the midday heat amidst smells of cooking and distant clatter of forks on plates, people eating brisket and dipping crusty bread in tomato juices and slurping wine and dripping it on their shoes to reveal what was and what could still be if you choose to let it.

He chooses not. Not for him, this place of devilish indulgence. He will find a wall by the town square water pump, where he will sit till the train comes to take him home. He will wash this place off his hands and out of his hair and face, he will drink water to nourish and purify himself and remain fasting, also good for the soul to remind him of the Christ within, who was also tempted by the devil.

"Christ must weep at the sight of this place" he mutters to himself as he shuffles through the scorching sun, lingering in the shade of the wide-spreading trees a little to catch his breath and swallow his thirst, then on towards the town square and the sun and dust and silence and emptiness, surrounded by happy families eating and drinking and discussing choice and flow and God and thanking for their abundance.

* * *

He sits. He stares at his shoe. He stares at the dust under it. He's home, his home till tomorrow, the low wall surrounding the square, leaning against the old trees or do they lean against it? All in ageing and easy harmony.

The water pump creaks as he tries feebly to get it going. A dribble comes out, then a torrent, gushing over his shoes, poor shoes, and up over his ankles as if determined to wash the dust of travel off him and welcome him to his new home.

Instead of seeing the pump's welcome for what it is, he jolts backwards cursing. Cursing for him, that is. No blasphemy comes from his mouth, but insults − stupid lazy idle (his favourites) pump, good for nothing just like the rest of this town of eating, drinking, snuffling pigs at their trough. A trough he wouldn't mind sharing now, even though he has promised a fast to Jesus. He regrets leaving the Station Master's house now − the food, though undoubtedly godless, smelled good.

He's hungry.

3

He sits, stomach empty and groaning, but with too much indignation at his plight to do anything about it. Truth be told, he's cross. Cross with God for putting him in this place, this day of the Lord, fasting, which is good, he knows, but within sniffing range of all these good-for-nothings stuffing their faces with him sitting on a wall under their noses, alone, with wet feet, and not even a sherry for his troubles.

"What's with the sherry?" he thinks to himself. Can't get it out of his head. The influence of this town. A spirit of drunkenness must hover here, and suck souls to its leery bosom. Well he won't be one of them. He resisted the wine, he certainly won't succumb to a sherry – a liquor he has only ever heard of, so no life-long longing or addiction to battle here. He is strong in his love of God and he will survive this ordeal.

And so he sits, shuffles his bony buttocks on the stones in a hopeless quest for comfort, as the clouds slip by, the day gliding into afternoon, still and gilded with sunbeams and birdsong. A beautiful day, if only he would look up and see it. Instead he sees virtue in penance. In keeping his head down to stare at dirt in punishment for his original sin, and that he may fly to heaven quicker than others when his time in this purgatory is over.

It's all a competition with him. Who is meekest, who is most penitent, who does more or less or this or that. Nothing ever taken at face value, loved and appreciated for what it is. It's got to be first to do this, best at that. Always to do with denial though. His mantra – less is more – but not promoting a seamless style or beauty, just less of everything other than lack. Plenty of that. They are abundant in that. There we are – they, or just him now, are in the flow! They have, or he has, all the lack in the world. See? God gives you what you desire, and plenty of it.

He still thinks of 'they' and 'us', not 'I'. He forgets momentarily that he is alone now, and that is why he is here. The reminder is like a soft thud to his empty belly, like a cat just landed on it.

A cat. Like this white one here, come to wind its way around his ankles like a fur-covered snake. Its purring resounds loud and vibrating into his ankles and it feels good. For a moment he indulges and enjoys. Then comes to his senses and weakly hoofs the cat away.

It elegantly side steps and looks at him with pity, then sinuously waves its backside at him and, tail in the air in the shape of a question mark, sashays off across the square in search of easy morsels.

For a moment the old man sags. A fleeting thought – enjoyment feels good. The cat felt good. How can that be wrong? Is it wrong? Doubt again, worming its way deeper. Has his whole life been one long choice to be in misery rather than a choice to look up and see stars, and feel the softness of a cat's fur and enjoy the gentle, cradling warmth of a summer afternoon? Why all this denial? Why not enjoy God's natural bounty?

His eyes close and he slides off the wall to the ground. He nestles himself against the wall, feet stuck out in front of him, the dappled light of a big old tree swaying like rippling water over his body, and slowly, gradually, he drifts off to sleep. To enjoy an idle nap in the afternoon, in the balmy scented air, with the distant lullaby of tables being cleared, and coffee being brewed, and bedroom windows thrown open and shutters closed for everyone else's after lunch snooze.

The town sleeps through the hottest part of this Sunday. Even the birds are silent and napping. The white cat, across the square, stretches out on a patch of cool grass, one eye on the old man, the other closed in rest. All is quiet and calm and peaceful and soporific.

He dreams. He is at the foot of a long flight of stairs leading up to the church, perched on the highest spot in town. It is shaded by trees so it is not too much of an ordeal to climb it in the hot sun.

He plods upwards, weighted down by his heavy coat and his dark and dust-laden clothes and luggage, but he carries on. It occurs to him to leave everything and carry on up unburdened by clothes and bags, but he doesn't unburden himself. He toils up one step at a time, heaving his bag up, dropping it heavily on the next step, then heaves his feet up after it. Then bag, foot, foot, bag, and on and on and getting nowhere. The church is still as far as it was before, but now he can see people milling about there, outside the doors, chatting to the priest and amongst themselves.

Someone comes down the stairs and offers to help – reaches out a hand to take his bag off him and he is happy to let it go. Already his step is lighter and he can move faster and more easily. They don't seem to be having any trouble with the bag. Maybe it's because he's old.

He is now gliding up the stairs. A sense of freedom fills him and he takes off his heavy coat and throws it aside, and it's like he's flying now, up and up, flying and floating and soaring up these steps that only seconds ago seemed so hard to negotiate.

Upwards he soars, towards the people and the festival atmosphere outside the church, and suddenly he is there amongst them, his feet still off the ground, and someone is circulating with a tray filled with little glasses of deep amber liquid. It is offered to him and he takes one – the liquid glints at him, as if winking, and he sips it.

Molten amber! Warm golden nectar! Sherry!

He laughs, delighted to have finally tasted this liquid delight, and everyone laughs with him and they raise their glasses, for they too have sherry, and toast his new arrival at the carnival.

"Life is a carnival, welcome to the carnival" they are saying, and cheering, and laughing, and there is a band playing somewhere as if saluting his arrival, just like when he stepped off the train.

The train. This town. Something discordant strikes him, and he looks down and there is his bag again.

He sees the sherry glass in his hand, and hastily dumps it back on the passing tray.

And he is gliding down the stairs, his heels dragging and hitting the edges of the steps, falling backwards in slow motion, away from the party, down to the dust at the foot of the staircase, and – bump – back to earth.

He wakes with a start, his head on the floor, making contact at the end of his slow sideways fall.

Disorientated, he sits up and glances around. Did anybody see? No. Good. Very undignified to fall asleep in the town square like that, like a common drunk.

Drunk. Drink. Sherry. Yum. He can still taste its slight sweetness counter pointed by the sharp, clean blade of the alcohol, and then the slow honey glide down his throat – ah, bliss. Heaven in a drop.

He catches himself, sprawled on the ground, dirty, dreaming of booze. What on earth? What must people think? What would he think if he saw himself like that?

"Dear Lord," he starts, "help me survive this place of fiends and temptation. Let not the devil get a foothold in my soul with dreams of hardship and smells of cooking."

He gets God's answer pretty quickly – he hears a chuckle in his head. The words 'enjoy it, I have prepared this banquet for you' pop into his head, followed by an image of brisket and salad and crusty bread and wine and coffee and ripe peaches dripping juice down his fingers, sweet nectar, and biscuits to dunk in the after-lunch sweet wine that looks and tastes much like sherry.

"Here we go again!" he thinks with a jolt.

"Why? Why me? I'm not a saint that I should be so tempted!" but the words spark a little flame of pride in his bosom, and the thought that maybe he is a saint and this is his testing ground, flutters in and lands in his heart.

An arrogant smirk breaks out, and is quickly subdued. He must remain humble, he thinks, but then, again – God's chuckle. "Just eat the food and drink the wine and relax. You are beloved and it is time for you to let go of your purgatory. It has been your true friend all your life, but it is time to move on. This is the place, this is the time, let go, rest, relax, enjoy the carnival of delights before you."

He swings his head this way and that, trying to find who is playing tricks on him, who is whispering these words of temptation into his dirty ears, but there is nobody, no serpent of deceit, curling and coiling its way around the tree trunks, no devil prodding him with his pointy fork.

Just a procession of children of graduated sizes, led by the Station Master's wife, carrying plates of food and a small carafe of wine, glasses, cutlery, bread, salad, heading towards him from the station.

They surround him with their banquet of delight and the children clatter their charges down onto the ground and the wall around him.

"We thought you'd be hungry, nobody goes hungry in this town" says the wife, as she pours him a glass of sherry – sherry! "I assume you don't like wine." And hands him the glass.

He looks at it. The sun bounces off the shuddering surface, and it winks at him.

The children stare at him in their innocent curiosity, waiting to see how he will react to their surprise visit.

He looks at their upturned faces. One by one – pink cheeked, well fed, well dressed, smiling. His children had smiled like that when they were young, but soon enough that joy was lost as they set out young on the path of penance.

"For their own good" he yells inside his head, but these little things, they look like cherubs. Can it be wrong to smile and laugh if it makes them look like angels?

So much confusion! He takes the sherry and in one swift motion drinks it, as if God has had enough of waiting and has taken the old man's hand and done it for him.

There. Mmm. Nice. Nice slow burn as it glides down his throat and releases the tension there. Softens his vocal chords so he can unwittingly let out an 'ah' of delight.

The Station Master's wife smiles, satisfied she has made the right choice, and pours him another.

Meanwhile, the children get busy. One puts brisket on his plate, another hands him a plate of salad – tomatoes and fennel glistening in their scented dressing – and another breaks off a hunk of crusty, crumbly bread and puts it in his hand.

The smallest child, that one. His mother pulls him away a little, as if to say 'let him break his own bread' but the deed is done. The old man has food in his hands and at his feet, accepted without his interference, and now he is temporarily one of them. Eating his Sunday lunch in this easy place, where if you don't go looking for abundance, it comes to you.

4

A larm bells. A siren in his head. It goes off insistently and piercingly, on and on and on.

"Why now?" he thinks. "Why me? Here? Now? Eating this food I didn't ask for" (but he did) "and drinking this wine I despise" (but he doesn't). He calls out to God to help him through this ordeal, knowing in his heart but unknowing in his mind/ego that it is God who put the bread in his hands and raised the glass to his lips.

God has stopped him in his tracks and made him sit down and have a bite to eat and be grateful to those around him, those he looks down on with his arrogance and sense of superiority-through-denial.

"Why?" he thinks. "Who would have thought that I, I, of all people, would end up sitting in the dirt eating a stranger's food and drinking their wine like a beggar, a tramp, a good-for-nothing idler who has wasted away their life in idle pleasures and wandering the paths of nature to do nothing but listen to birds and watch sunrises and sunsets and then shuffle into the nearest town to beg for his supper, instead of doing an honest days work and then sleeping the sleep of the just after a restrained meal, on a slightly empty stomach, kept that way for good, for nothing fills us up but the Lord?"

Phew. That thought was long and hard. Made him hungry. He takes another bite of bread and forkful of brisket – it's good – these peasants may have no brain cells between them but they know how to stir a stew.

Meanwhile the children look on, watching the funny mumbling old man scarf their food down, and they shove the plates and bowls a little closer so he can take more, like feeding an animal at the zoo, with all the fascination of seeing how one not of our species deals with everyday tasks such as hold a spoon, and eat a tomato. They gaze open mouthed until their mother, by now a little embarrassed at their open curiosity, tips their mouths closed and with a glance tells them many things – sit up, stop staring, stop pushing food at him, yes he's strange but he's still a human being, and sit up again, for good measure.

Well trained in obeying their parents, they all close their mouths and sit up and stop pushing the food at him, and try very hard to stop staring, but that's not so easy, because his muttering has gained in intensity while the eating carries on full throttle, and the result is food spraying everywhere, morsels catapulting from his mouth out in front of him so that his legs and coat front are peppered with it like he has been shot at with a food gun.

The Station Master's wife can't contain a small involuntary grimace as one especially large chunk shoots out of his mouth no sooner has it been placed in it, and tumbles down his front and into his lap, just missing landing back in the plate it came from. He simply picks it up and pops it back in his mouth mid-mutter, unaware of anything being amiss, and of the stares laced with mild and titillating horror that he arouses in them.

If he had any idea that they regard him as one of life's unfortunates, as a tramp who has wandered the world meeting obvious misfortune after obvious misfortune, and has never had the benefits they have lived with; if he knew they thought of him as someone who has never been taught manners and has probably never eaten at a table or with a fork and knife before; if he knew the pity with which the Station Master's wife was regarding him now, pity reserved for the destitute and ignorant and hopeless and abandoned by God (not that she believes anyone is ever abandoned by God – they simply refuse to look at him for a while till they come to their senses), he'd be so horrified as to probably have a fit and die right here on this now much hated spot.

He, who sees himself as vastly above these people, who sees them as ignorant and to be pitied in their easy harmony, he is the one to pity their un-knowing and un-connection with the divine.

And as this silent exchange of opinions and, on his part, judgement, continues, God smiles because he has got him to eat and drink and stay on this spot for now.

And that is the important part – he has to sit here for a while longer, because this is where he will reconnect with his lost family. The reconnection may not be wished for on their part, and the wish for it may now be denied on his, but it will happen nevertheless, and in the meantime he can eat and drink and start his reconnection with humanity in general.

"Ah." Sigh. "Good. That was good." He will go so far as to admit that to himself. Probably not so far as to admit it to the woman, sitting there waiting for compliments for something he didn't want and certainly didn't ask for.

She sighs. "Ah. Good. He's eaten. The Lord only knows where he comes from and where he's going – obviously all alone in the world to look and eat like that, and obviously penniless to look like that, probably never done a day's work in his life, but that's what the Lord has led him to do, so there must be a purpose to it. Wonder what he's doing here? Wonder if we should offer him a bed for the night? The boys can all bunk together in one room – they'll like that, an adventure."

But she's unsure how to broach that particular subject. He seems so gruff and mannerless that she's a little afraid to ask him if he wants to sleep at her house till tomorrow's train comes to take him who-knows-where.

He's wondering, now that he's eaten their food, are they going to stay here and sit with him, or are they going to demand money for food he never ordered? He'll soon show them who's boss if they try that one, and he starts to formulate angry and assertive replies to her inevitable demands for remuneration, but the food and the wine are drawing the blood from his ever chattering brain, and as his life blood flows towards his stomach to digest his lovely if unappreciated meal, his mind quietens a bit, and his eyelids start to close, and he snuffles a bit and places his hands on his belly as if to re-experience for one last time the pleasures he has just consumed, and then he is asleep.

The children are still staring, and their mouths have begun to hang open again in fascination at seeing this bizarre creature feed and snuffle and grumble and spit (they loved the spitting – one morsel travelled as far as his feet!) and now he is in the land of animal-sleep and they would dearly love to prod him with a stick to see what he would do – would he leap up and snarl, would he scream and chase them, would he try to devour one of them? – but they don't dare try this because they know what trouble they would be in from their mother if they did.

They worry a bit that she might be reading their minds and know their new desire, since she often seems to be there inside their heads telling them to 'think again, young man' as they are plotting some new childish prank. She, however, is lost in a reverie of her own, also staring at the old man, and wondering if she should bring a cushion to put under his head and one for under his backside, or whether she should deal with the bed-for-the-night issue now and wake him and take him home for his nap, or just let him be.

And so he sleeps, watched by cherubs, and protected by the mother whose only thoughts are about how to make his sleep better. Blessed place, blessed people, blessed old man who has found his home.

* * *

And so the day wears on, the heat intensifies and starts its slow and easy decline into cooler evening, and still he sleeps on.

The children have been joined by their friends and all play in the square, urged to silence by their parents who now sit a little further along the wall, chatting with the Station Master's wife about their strange new arrival. It seems all the town has turned out to watch him sleep off his feast.

The conversations are many but on one subject only – him. Where has he come from, who is he, why is he in such a state (clearly none recognise a pure life led in penury and penitence for the glory of God, as he would think were he not sleeping off the huge amount of food he managed to ingest in spite of the projectile spattering of it that he sprayed his surroundings with).

All are here bar five. Some of the townsfolk know the woman and her daughters left their old life behind and came here to find peace and happiness, and many were astonished to see the pleasure they took in the simplest of things – open windows with flowers in a vase on the sill, eating peaches in the middle of the day, just because they wanted to, having visitors drop in for a chat and a coffee and biscuits, and clothes, such pleasure they have in their pretty clothes, as if this is the first time they have worn dresses!

Very charming, all this delight in God's bounty, but a bit strange too. Did they come from such a place of denial? Nobody knows because they don't speak of it, and nobody wants to intrude on their privacy and ask, but nevertheless, all do wonder.

And now this strange beggar arriving, all rage and hunger and thirst and spitting and exhaustion and an air of misery and denial and loss and despair hanging around him like a curtain about to fall and smother him, his strange darkness somehow chimes with the five women's lightness and delight, and all wonder if this is the denial and despair they came from, escaped from, and now it has hunted them down and found them and is gathering its strength for the final onslaught, the final attack which will bring them down, bring the curtain down on their short-lived life of delights and drag them back to the tenebrous life of misery they were born in and will die in.

All look and wonder and pity the old man. All ponder and wonder and pity the five women. Are they linked? Is this their fate come to get them? Should someone warn them? Should they help them flee? Then –

They are five for goodness sake, four of them young and strong, and he is one, old and feeble and asleep in the dirt. They can take him. They can defend themselves can't they? Maybe it is they who will drag him kicking and screaming and spitting his food out like a baby, drag him with his child-like dirty face and filthy clothes from rolling around in the dirt ("he even has dirt in his ears!" they whisper), drag him into their world filled with light and flowers in vases on windowsills and scents of pea blossom and cake cooking and clean linens. They'll wash him and his clothes, dress him up in clean underpants and comb his hair and trim his nails, and sit him in front of the open window to breathe in fresh air and see his new world pass by while they iron and brush down his newly cleaned clothes, and someone will give him a pipe and slippers and he can glide gently into his dotage in a comfy chair, not in a gravelly square with his head resting on stone.

5

All are here, waiting to see what will happen when he wakes. What will happen? Will he rage and mutter and mumble again or will he run at them, ranting like a madman? Or is he just a tired old tramp sleeping off an unaccustomed big meal, and has nothing to do with anyone in this town and did in fact get off the train (or was thrown off) at the wrong stop?

All wonder, all wait, all watch and chatter amongst themselves and have a thoroughly nice time. The children play on as the light dims and the bar on the square flicks its lights on, dancing strings of soft colours bobbing like garden fairies in the dimming day. And drinks and snacks are ordered and the town musicians pluck a little at the strings of their fiddles and guitars, and an impromptu tune is struck up, and the place glides into an easy carnival feel, all happy and eating and drinking and enjoying this summer evening to soft music and lights and fireflies bobbing and dipping and flashing their glow into the balmy evening air.

This is when he chooses to wake up. In the flow of the carnival he dreamt about. He rubs his eyes, wondering if he has woken into some weird dream within a dream, but then the stiffness in his back tells him it is real enough, and he lets out a small groan as his spine creaks itself back into place.

Heads snap around, children and musicians fall silent, and all eyes are on him. He feels the pressure of their stares, and glances around in a growing panic. Are they going to attack him?

The Station Master's wife descends on him and he holds up his arm to ward off the inevitable blows, but she takes it as though he were proffering his hand to shake, and heaves him to his feet. This takes him so much by surprise that in an attempt to duck the assault, he leaps to his feet, helping her in her task so effectively that they finish the manoeuvre with a little jump.

Both land startled, but another town's person has joined in the help-brigade, and has deftly slipped a chair behind him, knocking the backs of his knees, which fold and buckle his legs, and he sits down abruptly. He is safe.

Silence.

Then cautiously, the Station Master's wife makes to speak, but is hushed by a wave of whispering and excited glances up the hill. Everyone's head swivels in the same direction, away from the old man and up the hill where a small procession of five women in pretty dresses ambles down the road for an evening stroll.

They are coming, as they do every evening, into the town square, to the bar, to have an aperitif. If it is an especially pleasant evening they may linger and, even though they have not yet had their supper, they may have an ice cream.

All watch and wonder – are they connected to the old tramp? Will there be a scene? Will there be tears and fists flying? Will there be name calling and will the men have to rush in to separate them when they become one big bundle of flying limbs and slaps and hair pulling? Some of the men roll up their sleeves just in case. Better be prepared for any eventuality.

Or will there be a huge sigh of disappointment when, if, it turns out they have no connection, and all the afternoon's chattering and theorising was completely wrong?

Who knows? Not them, right now. Nobody but the five women strolling calmly, unknowingly, down the hill, towards and into the waiting arms of their destiny.

For of course there is a connection. Of course it is they, his wife and four daughters, all looking prettier and younger and more like the angels they once resembled than he has ever seen.

Because he has seen them now. All are silent, and all heads have snapped back to him as the town holds its collective breath and tries to read his face, his thoughts – were they right? Are they connected? Will there be a fight?

He struggles to get out of the chair and seems to want to flee, but he is still stiff from his rocky bed, so movement doesn't come easy yet. He shuffles and tips the chair, and it falls over sideways taking him with it, and he is there, sprawled in the dirt ("this is becoming a theme!" he thinks) as they stroll smiling into the square, and into a sea of gazes, and into a reunion that in their minds is neither wanted nor blessed.

They stand at a distance, horrified to see him brought so low, dirty, dishevelled, rolling in the dirt. He is horrified to catch their eye as he crawls about trying to get to his feet, acutely aware of how he seems to them right now, on his hands and knees to them, at their feet, a beggar come for forgiveness and to plead to be allowed to rejoin the family, to be held to its bosom once more.

He has absolutely no intention of apologising and begging and pleading for anything at all, whatsoever, nothing, not a single thing, and he is furious, raging, that he appears supplicant. Him? Supplicant? Ha!

So he pushes himself upright, does his best to square his shoulders, and takes a deep breath to start admonishing them, but instead sucks in a grain of dirt from his grovelling, and starts to

46

cough and hack and choke, so they are forced to come to him and slap him on the back like they are winding him.

Someone brings a glass of water, someone else pushes the damned chair behind his knees again, and once more he is sitting in it with women staring down at him.

Breathe. He manages a less ragged breath as the grit grinds its way down his oesophagus and into his gut, leaving him feeling raspy and sore. He tries to speak but it has done a good job on his throat, and he croaks, and the pain is too sharp and sudden to allow words to come out, so he shuts up.

For once. For the first time in front of his family. They have never seen him silent before. He always had a torrent of complaints and dictates and orders and criticisms pouring from him like a river in spate, so that they grew to hate the sound of him. Now they watch him splutter and cough and croak, and quite like this new sound of speechlessness that emanates from him.

So they watch as he recovers, and all watch them watch him, and they and their audience have time, in this gap between words, to wonder what will happen next. They don't want him with them, they are much too happy now to want to go back to the way things were – but he is theirs, they can't

47

abandon him, turn their backs on him in front of the whole town. How would that look?

They look at each other and register their common dismay at the sudden change in their new and shiny circumstances, and a common resolve is born in that moment to not allow this belligerent old fool to spoil everything again.

They have a shed in their garden, down by the orchard. A little stone hut once used to store wood. It's big enough for a bed and a chair and a water stand. He can stay there tonight till the train comes to take him home tomorrow. And if he misses the train because he has regained his voice and has been too busy ranting (to the shed walls, because he's not coming in the house) then he can stay another night, till he finally does catch a train to carry him out of there and back to who-knows-where and they can continue with their happy new lives, not that he will be allowed to disrupt them even while he is here, because in their absence from him they have grown strong, and the distance has shown them how wrong he was all their lives, and how they were wrong in allowing him to make bad choices on their behalf when they should have been making their own choices all along, good or bad, no matter which, but made by them, not for them.

They spent years living with their mistake, and paying for it, and they are not about to go back to that. They'd have to be fools to be shown the error of their past, have that painful light of clarity shone on all the things they did wrong, all their bad decisions, and now having righted the wrongs, fall back into them. No. They are not fools. That will not happen. They are on the right track now and they are staying on it. He can tag along, at a distance, but he will not waylay them or ambush them or distract or misdirect them, because they have seen him coming and they are prepared.

They are strong now. They can take him. They'll take him home, wash him and his filthy clothes, feed him, give him a bed (in the shed) then send him on his way.

Phew. Breathe. That's alright then.

6

All is quiet as the women take him by the elbow, haul him upright and dust him down. A long stare – the wife looks him in the eye, for the first time without fear of his anger or his retribution doled out 'for their own good', and she tells him he is welcome in their house (their shed) for one night till the train comes, then he must leave.

He wants to shout and rage and roar at her – how dare she speak to him so insolently in front of all these people? – but he has not found his voice returned to him yet. It is still held prisoner by the gravel scratches and soreness, so he croaks at her, and it is taken as consent, and he can do nothing to correct that misinterpretation of his intent.

So he allows himself to be led by the now much less smiley procession of daughters and wife, away from the silent, watchful crowd, and up the hill.

His voice will return to him, he thinks, then they'll hear what he has to say. He'll give them what for, for speaking to him like that in front of everyone, all those strangers who first saw him as a drunken tramp and now see him as a weak, hen-pecked husband. How dare they?

He is choking on his rage, but his daughters take it as a continuation of the choking on grit and, instead of humble grovelling and apologies, he gets hearty thumps on the back propelling him all the way up the hill and into their pretty garden, and the walled off orchard, and into a stone wood-shed.

What the hell?

"This is where you can sleep" says his no longer subservient wife. She used to be such a good wife – never said a word out of place, did as she was told always, and now look – she's telling him to sleep in a shed!

He wants to roar at her; instead he flinches as one of his girls takes the bag of woes out of his clenched fist and drops it in the corner.

"We'll put a bed in here, and a chair and a water jug and bowl and you'll be fine. You can eat with us in the house." says one of them – he's too shocked by their disrespectful behaviour to notice which one, but by the time he turns to look, they are all trooping off across the lawn and towards the house.

It is a very pretty house – he hadn't really looked at it as they arrived, too busy coughing and trying to survive the battering to his poor back – but now he looks, he sees all the little touches they had tried to bring to his house, and which he had quickly put a stop to. Vanities that can only offend the Lord, surely.

In that moment he prays for them, having seen how far they have fallen from their path of suffering for salvation.

He prays they be forgiven the lace curtains fluttering in the evening breeze, the big pile of peaches he can see on the kitchen table – such excess. He prays when he sees all the flowers they have, in every window, in coloured glasses and vases and pots and all manner of junk cluttering the place up.

7

"Choose. Choose what you want to eat, choose what to drink, choose this, choose that, choose choose choose. Why can't they leave me alone?" he shrieks in his head, because his voice is still mercifully (for them) silent.

They are doing him the unkindness of offering him a choice for his supper and he is so vexed at this display of abundance and waste that he is starting to choke on it again. Why not just one thing for all for supper? Are they showing off now? That's what they are doing – they're throwing their new life in his face to make the point of how happy and loaded they are.

Where are they getting the money to live like this? Then – sharp intake of breath – they must have jobs! What is happening to his world? His women don't work outside the house!

Well, they did when they lived with him, but only for the church. His wife did the Priest's books and the daughters – one taught at Sunday school, though that was not paid, but the parents would leave her little gifts every week, some for the church, some for her, food and meat and cloth and things they had that they would barter for lessons in faith for their children.

Now, he's certain his 'wife' is not working for any priest, not in her fancy clothes, and they probably don't even have Sunday school in this God-abandoned, immoral party-place.

He's right of course, they don't have Sunday school here because in this land their children all go to church with the parents and learn their bible stories from the priest, along with the adults, and get their lessons in life along with the adults, and so we have the future singing star and the happy family pet to show how well this works for them.

But the old man would spit on that concept if he knew about it.

Back to choices. He is sitting at their large kitchen table in their airy kitchen filled with the ubiquitous flowers and fruit and lace, and they are boasting of their wealth and excess as if it's a good thing. Pride pours out of them. Sinners. Their words?

"Would you like ham or chicken for supper? We have both and you are welcome to either."

He seethes in his unaccustomed silent world and croaks out "chicken please" through clenched teeth, hoping they got some of the disdain with which he tried to fill his words.

They hear – "chicken please" – a simple request for supper. All bile and anger rebounds off them in their peace and harmony, as if all this newfound happiness has grown a shield of light around them that bounces all insult, all negative thought, all misery from them and sends it back the way it came.

The disdain, certainly, bounces straight off them and whams right back at him, smacking him between the eyes, and he shrivels a little in unexpected discomfort when his youngest puts the cold chicken on the table in front of him and smiles.

Her eyes and face are soft and radiant, and she is beautiful in her floral summer dress. He has never seen her like this, and it touches his heart like an electric prod.

A lump rushes to his throat and he thinks he might cry; instead it dislodges the remaining blockage and, suddenly, cool air rushes into his mouth and down his throat and inflates his lungs, and he takes a vast gulp of air and blurts out "Thank you."

Activity in the kitchens stops. All are staring at him. He glances at them, and at his youngest, and at the chicken, and doesn't quite know what to do.

"You're welcome." says his wife. And gradually the clatter of plates and pots and glasses resumes, and a glass of wine is placed in front of him.

"We drink wine here," announces the wife. "It is good for the blood." He looks at the wine and at her, and nods. Doesn't trust himself to speak just yet, because the lump is back in his throat and making his eyes back up with tears for some unknown reason, and he's in terror they will spill over and he will look a fool, for the umpteenth time today.

As the pots bubble on the stove – no idea what's cooking – he is slowly but surely filled with a sense of peace and home. The rich, green scent of a soup on the boil fills the kitchen, the warm hug of bread baking makes him breathe in so deeply he can taste the yeasty, crusty deliciousness already, and his daughters mill about, laying out crockery, chatting, some even humming or singing the song played earlier in the square.

They are like a scene from a story, of a happy family, all grown up in love and bounty, enjoying the calm and comfort of a life well led, all loving, all one.

Yet they are not all one. Well, they are, but he isn't. He feels very much the outsider, is the outsider.

They are one unit, happy now as they should have been with him. He sees this, now his mouth has been shut up for him and he has time to observe in between his bouts of shouting.

It's as if all the time he was trying to teach them well, to lead them down the path of righteous sacrifice for Christ, to begin to pay back Christ's suffering and to emulate him, all that time with his talking and shouting to make himself better heard and to stamp his authority over them clearly, it's as if all that noise coming from him obscured him to the reality he expounded, that peace and harmony is where Christ is and that he was already there amongst them. He just couldn't see it.

Again, just like on the train, he is faced with the evidence that he might have been wrong, might have made disastrous life choices that led to misery for no reason, and he struggles to accept it. What a waste of life.

His head hangs and, in his silence, so unusual, they think he might have died.

One daughter takes his pulse, another flips his head up and stares him in the eye, and jolts backwards, letting his head drop brusquely when his eye swivels, startled, to meet hers.

His wrist is left to slam back onto the table as his girls step smartly away, and their fearful silence speaks volumes about how he might have once reacted to such easy physical interaction. But they are in their own world, their own home now, separate from him and his rage, so they compose themselves. They do not cringe in fear, rather they stand straighter, and carry on their business preparing the evening meal as though nothing was.

* * *

And so the evening passes. They have soup, delicious, and crusty bread, even more delicious. They have chicken and ham and salad (from their abundant garden, he notices), and the scents of the herbs and the bread linger in his nostrils and he inhales deeply to keep them there longer, deeper, as a reminder of what could have been.

The women chat easily amongst themselves and, occasionally, one will make a foray out towards him and ask a question, or an opinion, or somehow try to include him in the conversation, more out of politeness (they are impeccable hostesses) than out of a desire to hear his thoughts because they have had a bellyful of those.

No. In their new comfort and security, they feel brave and compassionate enough to reach out to their once-jailer and forgive, and try to make him feel included not excluded, because they remember how bad that feels.

They remember being shunned and ignored by the townsfolk in their old grey home, shunned because every gesture of friendliness or inclusion would be met with derision and a volley of rudeness and rejection from this foolish old man, in his belief in his own moral and spiritual superiority. He looked down on his neighbours like he looked down on his family, and so made strangers of them all.

Now the women refuse to propagate that behaviour, and go out of their way to embrace all, and make all feel welcome. As a result, the entire town has grown quickly to love them as their own, and even the old man feels the warm flames of rest and warmth and love flickering around him as the aura of their success soothes and settles around him.

He sits, replete once more, and gazes about him at the happy women chatting and eating as though he weren't there, and it's a good feeling, a happy sound, and he longs for it to come home with him. Tomorrow, when he has reclaimed his voice, he will tell them his plan, that they should come home now – enough is enough – and he will allow them to take their knick-knacks, since they so clearly make them happy, and he has to admit they make the place look pretty.

They will resume their old life as though nothing has happened, and they can be as they are here, it's ok, he'll allow it, blah blah blah –

"What a fool. Once an idiot always an idiot," he yells to himself, "of course they're not coming home. This is home. You have to stay here. This is to be your home too if you want your family back. In the shed if need be."

This sudden clarity startles him so badly he knocks his glass of wine over and the red juice shoots out across the beautiful white linen like a flash of arterial blood, pumping out of newly cut flesh.

The women jump and scatter to avoid its projectile speed, then someone gets a cloth and water, and the spillage is being mopped up and he is being told it's ok, not to worry, happens all the time, and though he has scarred their table, they are soothing him like he was a frightened child expecting a beating for an accidental breakage.

He watches the wine stain disappear under their deft hands. Another glass is poured for him, though he hadn't touched the first. He looks at it. Drinks it. Watches their faces register surprise at the energy and determination he puts into swallowing that glass of what he would once (this morning) have described as the devil's liquor, and feels a tiny prick of pleasure that they have noticed the first step towards his rehabilitation into his family.

He will become as them, not them as he, and get them, coax them, into having him back, taking him once more to their hearts, making him a part of this happy, easy clatter, this warm fug of family and comfort and hope and light and forgiveness.

They don't know it yet, and would be horrified to have their whole story laid out before them in one go, but they will take him back. He will be returned to them, although it was never he who left, and they will welcome that reunion, blessed reunion, blessed family, blessed pot of soup on the stove and bread in their guts, and wine spilled across the table like a blood sacrifice, putting to rest the old and heralding the new, ushering it in like calling in the spirits, the gods, the angels and elementals, to come and dance around the newly formed and bury the old, and survive all with grace and love and unity, since all are one and the same in God's love.

And God winks at them, at him, sitting there with his happy smile (a first) plotting his new life.

He feels God's wink, and glances briefly upwards, then assumes it's the wine doing its work, and takes another sip before finding his eyes drooping and his head sagging, and the last thing he hears before sleep takes him, is the sound of voices belonging to his beloved daughters and his marvellous, miraculous wife, whom he never realised he loved quite as much as he does.

Blessed be.

8

He stands from his little bed, a stranger in a strange place, surrounded by strange tight walls, and bangs his head on some protrusion. He yelps, rubs the sore spot, looks belligerently around him and, in his confusion of having just woken, can't figure out where the hell he is.

Then it starts to come back – his wife, his daughters, the wine – drunk! He got drunk and fell asleep. "Oh Lord, why me," he moans , sick to his soul at being so tempted, and furious that those benighted women were allowed to perpetrate this evil on his staunch soul.

"Why, God? How could you allow that to happen to such as me?" he grinds on. A brief image, a mere flicker, no more, flits through his head and he instantly dismisses it as the dreadful influence of this place, and yet it was there and is there again now, look at it, blasphemy – God, raising his eyebrows and saying "lighten up."

Not possible. What a place. Even God is tainted and swayed by it. The very devil himself must run through its veins.

He starts at a knock on the door and fear freezes his features, as though the thought of the Dark One has somehow summoned him up, so easy is it in this town of woe, so close to the surface lives he.

The old man goes towards the door gingerly, but before he can inch it open cautiously, it is done for him and a tray of coffee and bread and jam pokes its nose into his quarters.

"Morning" comes the sing-song voice of one of his girls. "Coffee" she announces, unnecessarily since he has already seen it masquerading as the fallen angel, poking its nose into his world.

He wants to berate her for being party to his moral tumble last night, but she smiles so sweetly, and enquires kindly after the quality of his sleep, and seems somehow to be oblivious to all that must have passed as to make him doubt momentarily that it happened at all.

And then the tray is on the bed, and then she is inviting him to come into the house to wash and have more breakfast should he wish to, and then she is going back out and across the garden, and the moment for recriminations is gone, like that, whipped out of his hands like the wind in a handkerchief, fluttering away without a care at his lost opportunity.

Blast.

He ponders. What now? Should he take the train and get the hell out of here? But he remembers last night, through the haze of two glasses of wine (and two sherries at lunchtime, don't forget those). It was nice. It was warm and pleasant to be part of the family again. It was novel, and wonderful, to be part of a happy family – something never before experienced. He liked it. He wants it again. He wants to stay and have it again tonight. He'll stay.

He sits on the squeaky bed and sips his delicious (inevitable) coffee and eats the fresh bread and fruity jam, and is surprised to find life is good right now. Huh.

* * *

Inside the house, the usual happy chatter is punctuated by thoughts, comments, questions, on how the morning will progress. The train comes in at eleven fifteen and they have to get him down the hill and into the ticket office and then across to the platform by the latest eleven o'clock so he can have plenty of time to take it easy, find a bench that is a little shaded by the sun, and relax before his journey home.

They will make him some lunch to take with him – chicken sandwiches and a bit of fruit and a small bottle of wine. They can spare a glass and a napkin to give him for his journey.

But they must hurry – time has a habit of speeding up when you wish it wouldn't, and they saw yesterday how slowly he is walking now and they have no means of transport, so they all have to come together and get a move on and get him homeward bound.

They have no idea he has other plans. They would be horrified if they knew what he was thinking – that he might fake a stomach ache or an injury to delay leaving, or simply announce that he will stay, assuming as always that he can do as he wishes and they will fall into line with his desires because that is what has always happened. This gives him a moment's pondering though – since seeing the change in them, he's not so sure they'll do as he asks anymore. They drank wine in front of him after all, and worse, made him drink it.

Hold on – his mind is in a constant state of flip-flopping this morning, one minute condemning them and the demon drink they forced upon him, the next luxuriating in the mellow pleasures their world has enveloped him in. "Make up your mind" he bellows to himself, inside his head of course, because the part of him that wants to stay, that likes it here, doesn't want to blow his chances.

He breathes. He sighs. What next?

"I'll tell you what next," thinks his wife, although not in direct response to his thought because she is not, and has no intention of ever being, on his wavelength. She has one simple desire this morning – to get him washed and dressed and out of her house with a packed lunch, and down the hill to the station, and get a ticket in his hand and a space on a shady bench, all before the train arrives, and then she will make sure he is on it and she and her four daughters will stand and wave him goodbye until the train is out of sight and he is out of their lives once more, and she can relax. Breathe.

That's her plan for today.

A man, a woman, joined by God, and now look at them. Couldn't be more different, couldn't have got it more wrong, the pair of them. But his mistaken choices haunt him more than hers do her, although right now...

* * *

A knock at the kitchen door – he holds his tray, empty, rattling a bit, and beams at them. Taken aback, they stare for a second, then come to their senses and someone takes the tray off him, someone else offers him more coffee and bread and jam, and all is normal morning activity again.

He notices chicken sandwiches being made, and a packed lunch being put together, and he assumes it's for him. He remembers his announcement to the Station Master's wife that he wanted to get on the next train, so she must have told his family and now they are preparing for his departure. How to tell them of his change of plan? No idea. Something will come to him. Better come quick because one of the girls is brushing down his coat and coming at him with it – whoops, they've got him out of his chair and his arms in the sleeves and the back door is open and they're all trooping out, with his lunch, and they're crossing the garden and they're on the road heading downhill, and it's faster than his arrival because gravity is pulling at his feet faster than it needs to, as if it too wants him out of here and, oh no, they're already in the square. Good grief.

The station looms there, like the doom of the world, glowering at him in its sun-baked, flower-clad whiteness.

He doesn't want this swift exodus but it's coming anyway and it's all going too fast, so he's left chasing it, unable to catch up and stop its vigorous progress. He has to do something. Just do something.

So he throws himself on the ground. There. Done it. Back in the dirt. Face down.

That stops them and their relentless forward march. They gasp and gather round, and pick him up and dust him down and ask "what on earth happened?" and cluck and fuss. Heaven.

He mutters and makes some pained sounds, as though he might have injured himself but is being too brave to give them details, and they fuss a bit more.

Then his wife looks at the station clock – ten fifty-nine – and hauls him to his feet and says they'll check his knees and clean up his grazed palms once he's on the bench on the platform.

The minute hand clicks round to eleven o'clock and at that moment the church bells ring out, starting up their series of chimes that now are like a countdown to him. He must turn his women back and safeguard his place here, for today at least before the clock reaches eleven fifteen and the next series of chimes, which will herald the train's arrival, and their strong minds and bodies combining to lift him out of the dirt and onto the train and out of their lives.

He must beat the clocks and their chiming and stay here, for today at least. One day at a time. One small battle at a time.

Know your enemy – time in this instance, fifteen full minutes of it – and you are halfway to being the victor.

71

He will find time, and he will use all means at his disposal to conquer it. Start with age. He is old, he has fallen over, he needs a minute to get his breath back. He'll take two. That's a start.

But they are young – they're having none of it. And hup! He's on his feet and on the move, with much sympathetic cooing and kind words, but on the move nonetheless.

He tries it again, tries to trip himself up and throw himself to the ground, but they've got him by the armpits now, and all that happens is that he takes a couple of steps in mid air, bicycling his feet like a toddler being swung by its parents, and then he is back on terra firma again, still moving fast (for him) in the direction of the dreaded station.

It's five past when they step into the ticket office. The high stone ceiling echoes back at them the clatter of their many feet and he is mercifully deposited on a cool marble bench while his wife joins the queue for his ticket.

He is pleased to see people ahead of her, people who ask a lot of questions, who can't just state their destination and number of tickets, but have to know if there is a restaurant car (no) and if the conductor will tell them when their stop is coming up in good time to allow them to gather their bags, because they have many bags, can the ticket seller see? (yes he will, and yes he can, although he doesn't really need to see), and on and on, the kind of muddle-headed, idiotic questions that on any other occasion would make him spit with fury and have to fight the impulse to manhandle these people out of the way so the world can be allowed to move on.

Now he thanks the Lord for them, wishes them well and simultaneously wishes them a bit more confusion so they will stay there a bit longer, but no, they have asked all they need to ask, and it's his wife's turn at the window.

She's bought his ticket in a flash and is scurrying over to get him already, like a streak of lightning.

Eleven-ten. Think. Pee. He needs a pee. She sighs, exasperated, and tells him he can pee on the train. They have lavatories.

In the distance, chimes. Too early, it's only eleven-ten! But it's not the church bells, it's the train approaching.

In the distance, coming in slowly and announcing its arrival way ahead so all can be ready, it rolls towards them with easy grace. Coming in like an executioner, come to take all life and hope from him with one smooth glide of metal on metal, rolling towards him like an axe blade on a sharpening wheel.

Suddenly he is flying towards his destiny, literally, as his biggest daughters get him by the armpits and run him, feet paddling air, across the tracks, across the path of the oncoming, although still distant, train, and down the long sun baked platform towards the spreading flowering trees where they drop him, and all pant and laugh, and his lunch is handed to him and he is brushed down a bit more, and his protests that all this jolting isn't good for him fall on deaf, happy ears, because they are getting rid of him.

The big, clanging train pulls momentously into the station, its looming bulk overpowering everything, and almost drowns out the church bells chiming the quarter hour.

He makes one last break for it, claiming to have left something (what?) behind (where?) but they grab him, tell him they'll post it, whatever it is, and then they are lifting him onto the train and finding him a nice window seat, laying his lunch out in front of him, and then they are outside again as the Station Master waves his flag and blows his whistle ("all chimes and bells and whistles, this place," he thinks) and they are waving as the metal monster gathers itself for its first lurch forwards, and all jolt, then it smoothes out, then jolts again, and his family are laughing as he is jostled, and waving, and he has to wave back and smile although he really doesn't want to, because he mustn't upset them now. Must leave smiling and happy, so they will remember him smiling and happy, and so maybe be pleased to see him when he returns. Tomorrow. He's coming back tomorrow. Yes.

And he smiles and waves and relaxes now he has his new plan, and though his heart aches to watch them disappear behind him, and see the rich pinks and reds of bougainvillea and dahlia and hibiscus flash by and away as he moves onwards, or backwards into his greyer landscape, he rejoices that his life has opened up, and he has a new plan for them all, that includes life and love and peace and wine and harmony, and all these pink and red flowers that seem full of God's harmony and love, and will be part of him now.

Not the greyness anymore, not the dead hand of his old life doling out un-pleasure and miserable denial. What was he thinking? How could he have believed that to be right?

Now he knows. Now all is clear. Not to his family, but to him. He'll have to show them. Teach them. For their own good, make them see that they are all meant to be together. What God has made let no man (or woman) unmake. He made them husband and wife, and so they will remain. He'll see to that.

And so the train rolls on, clanging, clanking and hooting out of that little town of miraculous encounters and reunions and laughter and music and back towards the landscape of gloom, and he feels himself drawn back into its greyness, and feels the folds of his skin sag downwards with the weight of it, and swears there, then, forever, that this is it for him. He's returning to his old home to pack up, and the next train he takes will carry him and all his belongings to his new home.

He'll deal with their resistance when he gets there, but for now all is well, all is as it should be. Thank the Lord.

And indeed all is as it should be. Wouldn't seem like it to the women, if they knew what was coming to them, but it needs to happen, they must go through one more purgatory to clear their path to hell, and then out the other side.

All will be well. All is well. Always was and always will be.

9

The old man. Old, he feels. Weary, he feels. Sitting in his grey house looking out at nothing much, just a dusty garden that he paved over because greenery and flowers were too pleasurable. He misses the abundance of nature around his wife's house. He misses his wife.

All around him are the things and tools and memories of their miserable marriage, so many of which she chose to leave behind because they held no love, no caring. They were symbols of the denial he had beaten them with for the length of their miserable union, and she understandably chose to leave them behind when she chose to move on from him.

He hated change, he thought others were idiots for always wanting to progress, move on, get more, when what they needed, in his opinion, to get to God, was less. Less excess, less talking and yammering (although you could not shut him up when he was holding forth on all this nonsense) and instead all everyone around him seemed to want was more more more.

Ah well. He certainly got what he asked for. He wanted less, he got less. Less family, less a wife, less of her cooking and cleaning and so on and so on and so on.

And now he wants it back. He sees the idiots' point (hasn't come round to admitting they might have been right all along though) and now he wants more wife, more family, more life in his dead existence. He's tasted it and it was good, and he wants seconds.

He was planning to pack up all his stuff and get it all on the next train back, but as he looks around him, there is little that appeals. He sees it now with her eyes – miserable accoutrements to a life badly spent – so he decides to emulate her in her departure, and decides to take nothing, just his clothes. That way, he can maybe fool them into letting him stay once more. If he turned up with trunks full of stuff, they'd claim to have nowhere to put it, and be able easily to turn him away. This way, with only a small case containing his meagre wardrobe, he can claim to be visiting and he can stay in the shed like he did yesterday. Problem solved.

At his end anyway.

* * *

At the other end, at his destination, something isn't sitting right. Change is a subtle energy – it floats around us like dust for a while before it settles into our being. We can feel it in the air, smell it, sense it coming.

And so it is with the about-to-be-invaded women. Glad to have him gone, they haven't managed to settle back into their happy routine. They are still jittery, as though he is behind them, and a couple of them have taken to spinning round abruptly as though he has crept up on them.

They saw him off on the train, they waved till it disappeared in the distance, and there isn't another train back today, so what's with the nerviness?

None can explain, but all are affected, and one eventually voices their collective fear –

"He's coming back, I can feel it," says the wife, and all hang their heads, and wails are let loose, and a palm slaps the table hard in an 'I knew it' way.

"What can we do?" says the eldest, "Should we move? Run away? Go south for a few months so if he comes back he'll think we've gone for ever?"

A chorus of approval from the younger girls rings around the kitchen. Their mother is silent, pondering their dilemma, her brows squeezed tightly together as though trying to pop a solution out of her brain like popping a pustule. But none is forthcoming.

"Oh Lord" is all she can come up with. But it's enough – he's listening, and he takes that as a request for help. He can see their whole story, wrote it in fact, and can see that his solution probably won't be to their taste, but it is the next step, needed in order to go up the rungs of her and their life progression, onto their next level, and finally to step out into the light and abundance and glory that is their final outcome, their purpose achieved, and it is not what they would ever have imagined for themselves, but it will be wonderful and loved and they'll ask themselves, incredulous, how they could ever have doubted and how they could have failed to see that this is what was coming.

Anyhow, back to the now, and that is not their vision or mindset or understanding of things. All they can see now is their plight – their bedraggled and depressing and bossy and downright awful father and husband on his way back to them after they had so successfully escaped his clutches. What to do?

"Nothing," the wife decides, "nothing. We will not flee, nor hide, nor cringe before him like we used to. This is our life, our home; if he comes back here we can't turn him away ("Why not? We can!" come the girls' cries) so we will put him in the shed like before, but he will not be a part of our lives since he is not a guest. He can eat and sleep there, and will do his own chores, and we will not serve him like we used to, because we have made our own lives and have not invited him to join us, so if he forces his way back he does it under duress and we are under no obligation to step back under his thumb. He can live in the shed, but that will be his home and this remains ours, and our lives remain separate."

There is a muted grumble from the bewildered and panicked daughters, and the fear still hovers that he will bully and coerce and somehow end up shoving his way, unwanted, back into their lives.

But their mother looks determined, and they remember that look from when she first decided they were leaving him, so they take heart and rally a little, and soon all is chatter about how they will deal with their unwanted but inevitable intruder.

Some comments are sensible – "No taking him morning coffee. We'll give him our spare coffee pot and he can make his own." Some are youthful and full of the excitement of their unexpected upper hand – "We can nail the door shut at night so he can never come out again!" – which is met with a stern look and an admonishment to remember courtesy and kindness, and never to say anything like that again.

The wife takes hold of the mounting hysteria and reminds the girls that they are to be kind and well mannered to him, always, and to remember he is their father still and always will be, and to respect that always, and to love him for that always, and to look for the good in him, look hard, because every one of us is God's child and he loves us all the same, and he knows there is a spark of goodness and divinity in us all because he put it there, and it is our task on earth to find that within ourselves and in others, and fan the flames of it and make it grow till all can see it and be drawn to it, so that we can be beacons in the darkness and show others how they too can find their light and shine like gold for humanity.

"Dear God" she thinks, "where did that come from?"

The girls look at her in silent awe, wondering the same thing.

God looks at her, nodding his head, saying "Nice job."

She shakes herself free of that strange and unexpected thought and clatters some cups to reconnect herself with the real world, and distract the girls from their open-mouthed staring. "I've done it now," she thinks, "I'm going to have to do as I say, or they'll never trust me again. I'm going to have to look for the good in the old bugger and I have no idea where to start because I've never seen it, in all the years I've been chained to him."

And then she remembers when they met. She could see it then. Lots of good, topped off with a mop of black hair tumbling over his piercing blue eyes that would look at her like she was a peach ripe for plucking, and squeezing, and tasting, and he was going to do it, and he did – oh good God.

She shakes herself free of that thought too, but can't deny, there was good in him, oh yes, it was good.

Her gaze wanders out the window and down the garden path and in through the door of the wood shed, and she sees him in his old bones and grey rags and need to reconnect, and feels pity. So little, he has become so small of mind and body, when he used to fill the world, her world, with his beauty and love and desire to live and be alive and share it all with her. What happened?

She has no objection, suddenly, to him coming back here. He can stay in the shed, in remembrance of what they used to be, of what he used to be, when he was still young and full of life and light. The divine spark shone bright then. He was the beacon we try to become. So what happened? He became extinguished somewhere along the way. Took a wrong turning, and slowly he walked towards a deepening twilight instead of towards the light, and it was so gradual he failed to notice till it was too late, till now, when he saw them on their light-filled road, having retraced their steps and come out of the dark and found their correct turning.

He is now starting to retrace his steps, he's looking for the right road, and she's his signpost, his indicator of where he wants to go and where he was meant to be all this time, except he was too busy looking at his feet, at his own dusty progress, instead of looking up and seeing that the light had faded from his day but was still shining brightly back the way he'd come.

Now he's looked up. Now he's seen the path. It's a way off, because he's travelled far into the gloom, but he can see it nonetheless. Now he's just got to get there. And he will.

And now he has, if not a welcome, then a tolerance waiting for him. He won't be turned away. He won't be shouted at or mistreated (not possible in that town of abundance) and he will learn to be like them, and undo his past and his old persona, let it unravel and fall around his feet, and step out into his new world in an entirely new skin, reborn, refreshed, reclaimed in the bosom of his family.

10

Today all seems good. All shines with a new light. A light of hope. The air seems jewelled and sparkles as he walks through it. He feels touched by angels as he gathers up the meagre possessions he feels inclined to take with him on this momentous journey.

He is in no hurry – the train leaves in the afternoon – so he strolls through his grey house, wishing it well, thanking it for providing shelter over their heads all these years, and telling it his plans – that he is leaving to be reunited with his loved ones.

The house creaks and groans as if wishing it too could leave and flee to brighter horizons, but it has a bright future right here, with new people who have the spark alight within them, who will come and light it up from the inside out, bring it to life again and give it the joy and colour and divinity it has waited so long for and now richly deserves. A day of hope and expectations and prayers answered and dreams pursued for them all. A good day.

He waits at his kitchen table, chores done, bag packed, now just the eternity to wait till he can walk down the dusty road and buy his ticket and watch the train roll in and climb on it, all fidgety impatience, and wait for it to trundle and clank and hoot its way back to them. Won't they be surprised!

* * *

Not so surprised. They've sensed his coming since he left, and now they are at work, making the wood shed a bit nicer, putting a little table in there for him to eat at, and one outside for meals during this glorious summer, for they aren't expecting his visit to be a fleeting one. They have even hung a little picture on the shed wall, and clouds of dust and cobwebs obscure the air around it as one of the girls sweeps the long-untouched corners free of accumulated dirt.

They know the time of his arrival, since there is only one train a day, and a debate is in full flow as to the pros and cons of going to meet him.

Pro – he's old and may need a hand carrying whatever he's brought with him; a kindness.

Con – that'll make him think he's welcome, and while they are indeed making him welcome, they don't want to put ideas in his head, ideas of a return to the old ways of him master, they servants.

Pro – just do it, he's an old man.

Con – oh, alright, whatever.

Not a long debate then. They'll meet him. But if they are going to do it, they must do it with good grace, not with surly looks and grumpiness. Also, it'll give them an opportunity on the trip uphill, when he's a captive listener and can't pretend to fall asleep to avoid listening, to tell him the house rules – no bossiness, he's living independently in the shed now, they are not all living under one roof, he must treat the shed as his home, and they'll provide him with whatever tools and bits and pieces they can, but he is to look after himself. They know he has money, so they will not be feeding him. If he wants chores done, there is a very reliable woman in the town who will work for him. And so on.

Little do they know.

And so the morning draws on, oh so slowly for the old man as he sits and fidgets and rechecks his bag, and oh so quickly for the women, who have no chance to savour their last few hours of freedom from him.

There is a general air of mopiness and bad temper about the girls as they have all sorts of visions about their impending change of circumstance, and none of them favourable.

They envision being forced to abandon their pretty clothes, losing all their friends as he insults everyone who calls on them, even the birds and the butterflies abandoning their garden as he whacks their flowers with his stick – why that image, nobody knows, because for all his grim misery he wasn't one to actually destroy nature, just never encouraged it.

Nevertheless, images of wanton destruction and looming, creeping greyness inhabit their young minds, till their mother shakes them out of their torpor and tells them, reminds them, that this is their home, not his, and they will from this day redouble their efforts to bring perky liveliness into their lives (not easy, since they've been going at it gleefully, hammer and tongs, since they got here), but nonetheless, they will bring sunshine and flowers and birds and bees and prettiness and sociability and extra extra life into this place now to a) make a point to him that this is how it is and it isn't going to change just because he has decided to come here, and b) to try and cram it down his throat and see if anything sticks, because since they clearly can't get away from him, they are damned well going to try to change him to suit their new personas.

Ah yes. The seeds of change. Its scent in the air, its fine dust, charged with the new, the miraculous, the unexpected encounter, the chance exchange, the new replacing the used, settling over it like a fine powder so it goes unnoticed at first, but soon builds and builds till a whole new form takes shape without anyone realising.

He's about to have the dust of the new settle over him. It's started already actually, and he can feel it, the subtle shifts in his belly, the need to move, the slight agitation of the senses, the way his eyes keep flicking to the clock as if trying to speed time up, make it rush headlong into the future like it did yesterday when he was being ejected from paradise. Yet today, when he is trying to get back in, it's crawling slower than slow.

He'll go to the station now. It's hours to go, but he can amble, and maybe chat to anyone he sees en route.

What?

Yes, strange, but he feels like chatting. The happiness at his coming new life is bubbling up inside him so that it's hard to keep it down, and he feels he'll burst open if he can't tell someone.

So he grabs his bag, shuts the house up hopefully for the last time, and saunters out into the sunshine.

A mother and her children see him coming as they walk down the road, and smartly cross over, but he calls out to them, scaring them.

"Morning, beautiful morning isn't it?" he yells at them.

The woman nods, fearful, and ushers her children faster along the road. One of them stares at the old man in terror, as if about to burst into tears, but the other is fascinated and would happily stay and listen to the old monster and watch for some bizarre change to burst out of him, because the child has picked up on the new strangeness and is intrigued.

But its desires are quickly thwarted as the mother shoves him down the road and away, quick quick quick.

Never mind. There'll be others. And there are. Two men stand on a street corner smoking cigarettes and chatting. He'll join them.

He shuffles up to them and tries again – "Morning, lovely day isn't it?"

Again the stare – mouths open – but the men are obliged by their masculine hormones to show a bit of bottle and not run away, so they look at each other and shuffle their feet and mumble "Yes" and hope he'll go away and wonder what on earth is going on.

"I'm off to visit my family," continues the old man "going to stay for a while, they've been begging me to visit so I thought I'd go, keep them quiet for a while." He smiles and tries a warm chuckle – he's heard people do that – but his throat is unused to such activity, and it creaks and croaks and tries to clear itself, and it sounds like he's hawking up phlegm and is about to spit.

The men wince and take an instinctive step back. They nod their heads in poorly disguised disbelief at what he's saying, and thoughts of pity flash through their minds, pity for those poor women who thought they'd got away.

They all three stand in silence.

"Damn, this chatting business isn't as easy as it looks," thinks the old man, "these two are obviously not very good at it."

So he nods his head in goodbye and, to their relief, moves off down the road. They're not that bad at it obviously, because the minute he moves off, they explode in a hiss and mutter and babble of chatter.

Unaware, he carries on down the road, a never-seen-before spring in his elderly step, and decides he will buy a gift, a gesture of 'hello' and 'thank you for having me' type thing for his family, and he dives into the tobacconist's.

Inside, the bell clangs as the door closes behind him, and he is instantly enveloped in the rich scent of tobacco mingled with scents of sugar and vanilla from the sweet jars. Dark wood drawers line the walls, holding who knows what treasures – he's never been in here in all the years, decades, he's lived in this place.

The proprietor emerges from the back, a broad smile of welcome on his face, which freezes in fright and confusion when he recognises his client. His glance skitters down to the walking stick, then briskly back up to the old man's face, and a visible anxiety that the stick may be used on his goods flickers across his now blotchy cheeks.

But he too is in for a shock – the old man would like sweets. A pretty confection for women. Something with colours women would like.

"What the...?" thinks the proprietor, but a client's request is a client's request, and he gingerly sets about pulling out boxes of candied fruit and sugar dusted violets and pastel coloured creams to show his unexpected and frightening new customer.

Sweets are chosen and wrapped, and since a dialogue has been started over sugared almonds, the old man grabs the bull by the horns and launches into his much needed chatting.

"I'm going to visit my family, they've been begging me to go for ages but I really didn't have time but now I thought I ought to, to keep them quiet – heh heh heh." It all comes out in a mildly hysterical torrent, but the 'warm chuckle' comes out better this time, not like he's preparing a spittle projectile.

The proprietor backs off, carrying the sweets like a shield and, smiling and completely unsure how to react to the bizarre outpouring of lies, retreats into the back of the shop muttering about "gift wrapping."

And then the old man is alone again, but it's getting better, he's getting the gist of this. Now all he needs to do is get the others to talk back.

In a flash the proprietor is back with the box beautifully wrapped, and a separate little box "for the girls, from me."

"How nice" thinks the old man, "it's working. My chatting has made him a warmer person too." He determines to do more of it and spread his joy all the way back to his women who, the way things are going now, will be overjoyed to see him.

At the ticket office, he becomes one of those people who can't just buy his ticket. Even though a queue has formed behind him, he believes they all need and want to share in his excitement, so he launches into his chatting again with the ticket seller, about how his family are dying to see him etc, etc.

Behind him, and therefore out of range of the strange and frightening new friendliness about him, a man waits. A man who knows him well and has been on the receiving end of his volleys of abuse a few times. He hears the babble of invented delights, of a family 'desperate' to see him and, coupled with making him wait in line when his train is due in soon, this nonsense makes him see red. A new line about how the old man's girls have always loved candied oranges, makes him pop.

"Your girls? What do you know about your girls, other than how to keep them chained up in misery till they had to run away to get any sort of ordinary life? And now you honestly want us to believe they're dying to see you? They'll die alright, of sheer misery at having to look at your miserable face again when they thought they'd finally got shot of you. A box of bloody sweets isn't going to make up for a life time of not being allowed friends or parties or to behave like normal people and just go out to play! Begging to see you, my…"

The ticket hall is silent. The ticket seller hastily hands the old man his ticket; the old man takes it and, his happy bubble soundly burst, isn't sure where his feet should take him; the people in the queue between the old man and the angry man shuffle silently forward and whisper their destination to the ticket seller; the angry man clamps his lips together as his face flushes arterial purple, and hopes he isn't going to have a heart attack.

All in all, the old man thinks he's given the chatting a good shot, and might give it a rest now.

He can't look the angry man in the eye. Once, in his old skin, he'd have leapt to his own defence and hurled high decibel abuse at him, punctuated by a waving stick, and a shouted lecture on manners

94

and minding your own business and the Lord this and the Lord that would have drowned out even the sound of passing trains. But now, he's silent. The words, though harsh and rude and none of the angry man's business, have hit home. He's going back to his family with no thought of their desires. He's never had any thought of their desires before, other than they should be suppressed for their own good, but now he thinks of them, can't help it, because even though he is still the same man on the outside, the dust of change has settled over him and, on the inside, he has begun the subtle shift.

He is no longer the same. He now is aware they might not want him back. He is aware he was going to force his presence on them because that is what he wants. He is aware now, that they ran away to be free of him, and that he should respect that. He is aware his happy bubble is now in the past, his rosy future too, and he is finally, drastically, fatally aware that he is not going to see his family today, not going to start a new life of light and flowers and home cooking. He is going back to the grey, harsh, dusty house and he is going to leave them alone, allow them the freedom they had to abandon all for.

It's a hard dream to give up, so he sits on the platform, on a shaded bench, and watches the minutes and hours tick by, faster now than before, and watches the train appear as a dot in the distance, hears the clanging and hooting as it announces its momentous arrival, breathes in the hot smells of its engine and brakes, and watches the passengers descend and be welcomed, and others get on board and be waved to and kissed and missed already.

He sees an empty seat by a window that would have been his.

The Station Master looks at him as he raises his flag, and gestures to him to get on, the train is about to depart. He even goes to help him with his bag. But the old man shakes his head and thanks him for the offer of help, but he's not going now. Maybe tomorrow.

So the flag is waved, the whistle blown, and the train moves on towards his to-have-been home, and he stays behind.

* * *

At the other end, on the bougainvillea and hibiscus-heavy platform, his wife and daughters wait. They have come to terms with his arrival, and have settled into an easy rhythm with it. They saw how a simple glass of wine was enough to loosen him up and make a human being of him, so they are taking him out to lunch. He will be made to behave, and if he tries to shout at anyone he will be told off and made to apologise, and if he won't, he'll be sent outside. But they don't anticipate trouble because he was different when he left. Something had shifted in him.

They are so sure of his arrival and subsequent good behaviour that they have booked a table at a restaurant off the square. The town's only restaurant, it has a lovely garden, tables shaded by an abundant canopy of vine and wisteria, and the colours and scents under there are enough to make a heart of stone sigh in contentment.

They'll have a long and easy lunch, and discuss house rules and how the future, their future together, is to be, and then no doubt they'll have to push him up the hill to sleep it off, because the other day one glass, or was it two, sent him straight to sleep.

And so they wait and plan and discuss what they will eat, and who will share what with whom, and as the train pulls in they scan the carriages and window seats and the groups of alighting passengers for their new guest, but see only others' guests and friends being welcomed. Their own is missing.

The last passenger hops down to the platform, and the train pulls out as all leave, cross the tracks into the station building and out into the town, and there is no remaining old man unable to walk fast and so left behind at the back of the crowds. Just an empty platform.

The women look at each other, bewildered. They were so sure – his arrival was a tangible force in the air, as if a fait accompli, as if he was already here. Yet he isn't. What has happened?

Slowly, they accept his non-arrival and cross the tracks themselves. They look at each other, as though the answer might be written on one of their faces, but it's not. No clue as to why things have not turned out the way they expected.

And strangest of all, they are not elated at his unexpected absence. Only this morning, they would have sworn that his change of heart would have had them dancing on the ceiling, but the subtle change-dust has been floating and settling around them too, and they have already become accustomed to the idea of a family reunited, under changed circumstances, with an opportunity for growth and developing into something good, their family being fixed and made whole. It had come to feel good, this chance for healing, and now it is vanished.

One of them, the youngest, is suddenly angry at him, furious, for thwarting them and their plans and their chance at new happiness yet again, but the outburst is quickly quelled –

"Something has happened," announces their mother, "he meant to come. I wouldn't be surprised if he was at the station hours early; he was going to come and something has stopped him."

Her mind has turned inwards – they see it from the furrows in her face – as she scans her mind and beyond for possible reasons, for what might have stopped him getting on that train, but nothing presents itself.

All through lunch under that scented canopy, she thinks and sends mind-feelers out into the ether, attempting to connect with what went wrong. Now she has seen her man as he was, a new desire has been born in her to have him back, to wash the grey and the old away from him and reveal the vital and alive once more, reclaim him and make him new again, and her first opportunity has been thwarted by she knows not what.

A decision is made – if he hasn't been able to come here, she will go there and get him, and bring him back, and make him stay and be changed and made new. He doesn't get away with it this time. Too long he thwarted her, too long he withdrew and pulled away and hid all that was good and bright and vital about himself, till when she saw him the other day, he was all but extinguished. But that tiny spark, the remnant of his once roaring flame, still sputtered when they put him on the train to send him home. She saw it briefly, not knowing what she saw, when he fell asleep at her table, and then when he battled so hard to stay, throwing himself in the dirt at her feet in his desperation (though he would never think to just ask).

Now she knows it's there still, she's going to go get it and bring it back and nurture and scrub it, and feed it and get it going again till he's alive again, for the first time in decades, till he's really, properly, fully, come back to her.

* * *

In the grey sad house in the grey sad town, he has no idea. Back at his table, arms resting in front of him, head too lost in failure to even have the will to slump, he feels emptiness fill him up – a vacuum sucking away all that was left of him and leaving a heavy, dark hole that pushes and sucks at his ribs and makes a desert of his soul.

A brief moment of resurrection, a glimpse at a new life, has had a devastating effect on him, and now all that was once his and fine and wished for and as it should be, seems vile and dark and empty and pointless, and every fibre of his body and soul strains and fights to be on that train, getting off at that station and hurtling up the hill to that house of flowers, to watch and gaze at his lost loves, his wife and daughters whom he punished and denied and drove away with his blind idiocy.

How did he come to this, when did things change? He remembers life before the misery started, and they used to laugh together. She used to smile, all the time, at him, by herself, at life. A long time since he saw that smile, but he saw it yesterday morning as she looked at her garden and her girls, and even at him. She's happy now and she was happy then, but in the middle, when he changed, so did she. He lost her then, and didn't know it, didn't see it, didn't see his life, his joy, his passion, running out of his life like water down pavement cracks. Couldn't see the broom of his fervour sweeping light and love out of his house, to disperse like dust in the air, never to return.

Except now, yesterday, he saw a chance for it to return. Saw it there in their cottage, and he wanted it. Wants it still. What to do?

What to do?

11

He sits swallowing his misery like cold tea, and ponders and allows his brain to spin on empty, and breathes in the dust, as the sun drops heavily out of the sky and crashes towards a horizon heavy with disappointment and loss of hope. The night ahead, not to be spent in a stone shed with the scent of grass and nettle and blueberry bush creeping between the stones, looms heavy and long and drear, and he dreads the slow tread up the stairs and the squeaky door into the empty, grim room and the view out of the window to nothing.

His grey life, until recently just fine, as he had wanted and planned, seems now an oasis of hope compared to this barren wasteland. His heart feels leaden, as though one tap would shatter it's brittle casing, and he hopes it'll happen, to take the edge off the hollowness he feels.

All is lost – life, love, family, and he cannot gather the energy for that pointless climb to that pointless bed for meaningless sleep, although the thought of oblivion is good, but he can get that down here. So he curls up on the floor and prays for an end to this day. Not yet a prayer for the end of this existence, but that hovers close, on this day of shattered dreams.

* * *

Similarly, in the house of flowers, his wife lies awake in her bed and ponders. She had expected to be lying here, thinking angry, bossy thoughts about him as he lay snoring in her shed. Instead she's fretting, concerned in case some injury has befallen him and, having nobody who is allowed to come near him without risking hurled insults and verbal violence, he could be bleeding to death with bones broken or head shattered by a fall down the stairs.

Ok. Get a grip. He just didn't show up. Changed his mind, that's all. Missed the train. No he didn't.

She can't sleep, won't sleep, not now she knows, knows, that something other than casual mischance has kept him from her.

Why would she want a return to the old ways? She must be mad – how does she know he'll change, that she'll be able to change him? She's not as she was when she was young, look at her, liver spots on her hands, more grey than blonde hair on her head now. She's old and isn't going back to her youthful ways, so why would he? Madness to bring

104

him here and risk all the misery starting up again, madness to ruin all they have built for themselves in the face of such hardship and denial.

But the germ of change has settled in her, the seed has sprouted, and is sending out shoots and feelers, groping for more, for progress, for growth, and she can't stop nature, can't stop the natural moving on that comes hand in hand with life on this earth and beyond – change plus growth equals life. Everywhere, it is so.

So she tosses and turns while her girls sleep and snuffle and grumble and sigh, gone who-knows-where in their easy sleep, while she stays resolutely here, wishing she was there, where he is, so she could see for herself what on earth is the matter.

No matter. She'll get the train tomorrow and go and find out, and sort him out, taking no nonsense from him because she is no longer the same person who lived in that house of gloom, and bring him back. She'll have to spend one night there, because she won't get there in time to go get him and catch the train back, but she can survive one night now she knows it's temporary.

* * *

If only he knew she was coming. He'd toss and sigh and feel his heart weep bitter tears with calmness, because he'd see its ending – that this is a phase, a passage, a purification needed to transcend his old life and step up into the new. But he doesn't know, doesn't see, and so suffers through an endless night when he thinks that emptiness might make him vanish into nothingness if he didn't feel so heavy, of heart, of body, of spirit. All feels dead and leaden and unable to move on from this spot of desolation.

He'd like to have the energy to get up and walk down to the river and throw himself in but he can't, he's rooted to the spot, to the stone floor, curled up like a cat, mind numb, body numb, here till he dies.

And then he wakes up. The sun is pouring through the window and he is in a sweat. His back is stiff and his jaw locked from its night-long contact with the stone floor.

He groans and yelps as he levers himself from the floor, and his mental anguish is forgotten in the face of his all new physical anguish – what was he thinking, sleeping on a stone floor at his age?

He clicks and cracks as he straightens up, or attempts to. His arm won't quite sort itself out, but – ouch – yes, there. Oh Lord, what a state.

He needs a bath.

* * *

He pours water from the stove into the tin bath and sets another pot on to boil. What a long and tortuous process. He should just throw himself in the river and be done with it – clean and dead. But what if he floated? He can swim, always could, from smallest infancy. He wouldn't drown if he can swim, would he? So that would be a waste of time.

But this interminable process with the pans, so small, and the bath, so big in comparison – the water in the tub will be cold by the time the next pot has boiled. Maybe he should just get in now.

So he strips off his clothes – all dusty and wrinkled now, where they'd been clean and pressed for the journey yesterday, damn it – and he touches a toe in the water. A bit of cold from the cold pail, and voilà, perfect. He steps in and sits in two inches of water. Not exactly a baptism.

But the touch of the water soothes and calms, his misery and heaviness seem lighter, and he sighs, "Aaaaah," long and easy and vibrating in his heart like a massage – "aaaaah" – again, like a hand caressing his heart and soothing and making everything a tiny bit better.

He settles into his puddle of bathwater and sighs and sighs, his contentment building with each one, his heaviness dispersing, as though his sighs were offloading his heart.

And so, when he hears an unexpected hammering at his front door, he is light of heart and clean of body and yes, even smiling to himself in spite of being wrinkled like a prune from his now excessively long immersion in his now armpit deep bath.

He sits up, stares in the direction of the door in astonishment, and has no idea what to do. He has never had visitors before, well not for the past however many decades, not since he started making it clear how he felt about all those who called (not flattering thoughts), so who would come and attempt a visit? Must be official.

He begins hauling himself out of the water, but the visitor has tired of waiting and has come round the back and is now staring through the kitchen window at him, wallowing like a fish in a pond in his happy bathtub, and she's furious.

She hammers on the window for him to let her in and, in his modesty, he trips over himself trying to get out while not letting her see his prune-like nakedness, although clearly she has seen it often enough in their years together judging by the number of girls she left behind today.

He trips over the edge of the bath, then the towel, and ends up careering across the kitchen head first into the door. Bang. His cranium thumps the wood and he bounces back, and sits down heavily on the floor.

Panicked, his wife rattles at the door handle and it miraculously gives way under her determined grip (miracle or dry rot? Who knows? Who cares?) Not she, as she hurtles to her husband's side as he sits stunned on the floor.

She checks his head for cracks – none. Checks his eyes for life – still there. So she hauls him up, wraps his modesty in his now damp towel, and glares at him.

"I came, thinking you were either dead or maimed or in some trouble because you weren't on that train as you were meant to be" (forgetting, of course, that he never said any such thing, just thought and planned it) "and instead you are here wallowing in your bath like a whale, happy as can be while I worry and plan our future like a fool, thinking we can be alright and happy again. A fool. What a fool."

They look at each other, and he is only now coming to his senses and realising she is standing before him. He tries, strains, to focus, and reaches a hand out to her, unable to believe it is her and not a hallucination borne of brain damage.

She smacks it away – it's her alright.

He blinks, and continues to stare. Her gaze softens when she sees his confusion, and she sighs. A big, heavy sigh, then another, and as she pulls up a chair, she lets out an "aah" just like he did earlier, and it vibrates gently in her heart and gives it a little massage, a small shaking that loosens some of the anger, sets it free to escape through her mouth, and everything is a little teeny bit easier.

They sit and look at each other, this couple who got it so wrong, and their hearts are a little softer, a little easier, so they can look at each other, see each other with a thinner veil of anger and pain and remorse. They can glimpse a little more of the core, the spark, of the person in front of them, he more than her, and so they take their first step on the path to redemption and forgiveness for their wronged union.

It will be a rocky road – it's not over yet – but at least they have started on their path, taken the first of a million steps that will lead to peace and harmony and a life of flowers and milk and honey that was there all along, but which they couldn't see, him more than her. But it's never too late. Never, never too late to turn back, see the signposts for your heart's desire, and set off on your journey towards it.

And that is what they are doing, as they sigh and soften their hearts to each other, and look, and see what is there rather than what masks what is there. And in their silence, pacts are made, to stay on track this time, to honour each other, to love, help and trust and be kind and true and willing to do anything to get it right this time. Vows silently renewed. Love restated and rekindled out of compassion and relief and recognition of what was and is and can still and always be.

Blessed couple, blessed bath tub, blessed gloomy house, whose spirits are a little lifted at the unexpected flowering of love within its walls.

12

He's there. She's there. Together after so long apart, in the same room and in the same heart space. The space between them was for so long so vast, a desert of annihilated love, but now, there is no space between them, they are one, whole once more as they were, and were meant to be always. Their separation has served a purpose though, it has made them clear in their heads about what is and isn't important in this world, and what is carried through to the next – they feel this one viscerally – and it is not denial and unkindness and judgement, but love. Only love. All is love. Understanding, compassion, kindness, tolerance, growth, learning, development into more than they were or ever thought could be, that all comes from love.

They know this now because these few hours spent together in virtual silence, just reconnecting and being together, has opened not just their hearts but their eyes and souls and memories, and all is renewed and refreshed and they are ready for a new go at it. A new start, a new life.

But first they must finish with the old. Tie up loose ends, tidy things away, bury the scraps and ready everything for a clean and smooth transition.

And that, old man, means making things right. He had a sense this might be the case – the shifting change in him whispered a warning of it. Nothing as momentous as this, this growth, this second chance, comes without having to tie up loose ends. Can't leave them flapping in the wind, waiting to catch and snag and ultimately unravel all the new good.

So, deal with things he must, and will. Now he's seen the signposts for his true journey, he's willing to spend a little time preparing for a smooth departure. Not looking forward to it, mind, but willing.

And, of course, the loose ends, the flapping things needing to be tied up and trimmed and fixed are all the people he has insulted and verbally assaulted and angered and hurt over the years of his intractable superiority and arrogance. Oh my, they are many. A whole town full, people who once were friends and neighbours and colleagues, who grew baffled at his sudden withdrawal of friendship, and then hurt by their punishment at the hands of one they once held dear.

Why did it happen? None of them knows or understands, and though some suspected mental illness or depression, and tried to ignore the vileness pouring out of him so they could try to help, all eventually were tainted by it, and one by one fell away, muttering that this was his burden, he would be the one to pay, not them, and slowly time passed and he become more and more isolated in his rage and fury. He didn't know where it came from, it just seemed to build in invisible increments, subtle, discreet, so the transition from happy husband, father and friend, to ugly rage-filled monster came softly, creeping, and hid him bit by bit, so nobody could gasp and grab him and force him to be helped. They saw no shift, no change – too delicate to be noticed – but one day, there he was, transformation complete, and he was unrecognisable from those earlier days.

Where did it come from? How did it get here? Why him? And how to be rid of it completely, with certainty that as soon as their guard is down, it won't creep back in?

Who knows? Not them right now. All they know is that some apologies must be made, so they can leave on a small note of reconciliation with people who didn't deserve his ire.

He won't ask for their forgiveness, can't give explanations since he doesn't yet have one, can only offer sincere regret now that his sealed heart has been prised open, and he has reconnected with the great cosmic heartbeat, and has seen that this is where it is good to be.

He wants to let his once-friends know, even though it is and has been clear to them for a long time, that they did nothing to bring his anger and contempt down on them, the blame was all his. They know this, but he wants to say it to them, not as an act of penance or humility, but as an act of love and apology. They didn't deserve it, and he wants them to hear it from his lips.

So between them, he and his renewed wife clean up his clothes and press them and make him presentable, ready to go around the town and knock on doors and present apologies, and in some cases receive forgiveness, in others a door slammed in his face, but always preceded with an apology to her, since they all hold her in pity and compassion for her burden of being married to such a man.

* * *

They see her walk with him now, arm in arm around the town, and wonder, once they have slammed the door on them, what horror he must have perpetrated on her to make her return after her so successful escape, and not only return, but endure the humiliation of traipsing door to door with her tormentor, carrying the burden of his vileness as if it were her own, begging forgiveness (for this is how they see it) as though blame was hers.

Nobody understands why they are doing this, what it is in aid of; many are confused by her presence, and a few think they see something which can't possibly be there – she'd be a fool to harbour it instead of giving it an almighty kick up the backside and telling it to clear off for good – they think they see love returned.

This last one baffles them most, much more than the bizarre spectacle of the bully begging forgiveness and doling out apologies like his life depended on it.

What is she up to? Now suspicion begins to fall on her, where once pity and compassion held sway. Is she turning too? Is she going to start with the hell-fire and damnation and kill-all-believers-in-anything-other-than-what-I-say?

Is that what this is all about? A new crazy fundamentalism coming out of him in a fresh, insidious way?

As they trudge around the town tying up and trimming, they can feel the suspicion and curiosity and masked and open hostility, but they carry on anyway. "A job that must be done," they say to each other, completely unaware of the wild suppositions going on in peoples' minds. They just see apologies and making things right. They don't see machinations and intrigue, and that even in good people there is a gateway to a darker place, always waging its small battle to get out and stretch and shout its name into the air.

With their display of moving on, of leaving their dark behind, the darkness living buried in others becomes agitated – is it too going to be cast out? It had better do something, and quick.

So the dark germ in us all (because there can be no light without dark, no good without evil, and all is contrast, all conflict, all mirroring of one thing against another, equalling life, always), that dark germ sprouts feelers, reaching out for life in its fear of sudden extermination, and in some, finds purchase.

In others, the glimpse of love borne out of such adversity simply serves to open their hearts more, and the germ has the light of the cosmic heart shone on it, and withers and dies. But in some, those who have held on to their righteous anger and hurt at the hands of this man, and don't feel he has been punished enough for what he did to them, and doesn't deserve his sudden return to the light, in them the feelers find grip, establish a small hold and climb and wiggle their little heads, trying to see an exit, so they can creep out and grow and flourish, just like they did in the old man so long ago.

These are the people who see conspiracy behind his simple apology, plotting behind her stance beside him. They invent and embellish this simple act until it gleams like a tacky Christmas tree full of cheap, sticky baubles, made up of invented innuendo and gossip and hate-filled fabrications of what his "sorry" could really, really mean.

This grey town has released one soul from its tyrannical grip of dour misery and suspicion, and spawned a whole new generation, all waiting to grow and spread their gloom amongst their friends and neighbours and ultimately their families, till they too become as he, alone and hoping for a new life away from all this.

Their time will come for the descent into the mire of their own creation, and then they too will glimpse the light of their heart's desire, left far behind, ages ago, and they too will have the opportunity to stop, look back the way they came, and choose to turn and head back that way, for God wants all with him, happy, showered with his gifts of love and light and bounty, but not all are ready to choose that way yet.

Some will trudge on into the hell of their own creation, unwilling to let go of their opinions. Believing they are right will have become so much more important to them than living in peace and love and riches of all descriptions, so that is what they will get. We get what we choose, and what we choose is what we fill our minds with, every day, moment by moment, thought by thought. Our choice, our gifts, our lives.

* * *

The old man and his wife choose life. They choose peace and forgiveness, and so that is where their tired feet are taking them, but not before crossing the final threshold, one last purification, a final clearing of all the dark germs and feelers and creeping vines that found such sound purchase inside them all those years. They need one last fire to burn it all to ashes so they can scatter the dust of the old to the winds and see it disperse, powerless and done with, and leave them clean and fresh for their new start.

This cleansing fire already crackles and spits, its first sparks lighted by the hissed comments and whispers behind the doors closing in their faces and on their apologies.

The sparks will run like wildfire and catch them up and consume them, and it will be terrifying and feel like a death, and it will be a death, death of the old, to reveal the new, emerging gleaming in the sudden clarity of a new day.

All must pass through this cleansing flame. All new life, truly new, has a test, a guardian to keep out those not quite ready yet, and to step through the terrifying gate of the new is a step not to be taken lightly or with the assumption of success, because if they are not ready, they will burn.

But they are ready. They don't know it, and they have no idea they are to be so tested on their resolve, but the new life is waiting for them, full of faith that they will pass the test and emerge bathed in the glory and glamour of the reborn, and so sits, patient, and watches and waits to see how the test will shape itself, what form it will take (gossip and innuendo will clearly have a place in it) and how and when it will present itself.

Poor people, to have this ahead of them when they have overcome so much already, but blessed, that the cosmos conspires already for their success, that it sees their ultimate safe passage through the consuming flames and engages its gears of change for their new future together.

Cursed and blessed town, cursed and blessed people who now have their own descent into hell and subsequent re-emergence upon them, cursed and blessed couple who thought it was all behind them but will find the worst is yet to come.

* * *

Blessed be. Blessed be stories with no beginning and no end, like the earth and the cosmos, always revolving and evolving and starting and ending and being reborn like an eternal flame.

13

Here he is then. Standing, alone in front of yet another door, because he's decided he can't put her through this again. It's not her penance, not her job to say sorry in order to move on, so he's sent her home, to old home, to be away from the slammed doors and odd looks. Only so many a person should have to take when it's not their crime they're being punished for.

So he waits for the looks and the odd glance and sometimes the insult and sometimes the kind word, as he carries on his round like a milkman carrying woes to disperse and set fire to – "bring out your woes, I'll see to them for you, bang! Gone!"

Except they're not exactly 'bang! Gone!' not in all cases. There are angry people who would like the phrase to apply to him, and look like they might just take a stab at making it happen themselves, so offended are they by his contrite appearance and assumption that a muttered 'I've come to apologise' is actually going to make it better after so much betrayal and rage and hurt.

Oh no. These folk are not going to give him an easy ride. If he wants forgiveness, he can go whistle.

But they've overlooked the fact that he hasn't asked for forgiveness, has in fact simply offered an apology. So he receives blessings for making amends, or trying to, and blessings for seeing his mistakes, and now starting the long climb out of his self-created hell, and it is they who bring the darkness out of its long hibernation, wriggling and spiralling up out of the soil of their souls and into a new germination. They, by their lack of forgiveness and newly reborn anger, give flight to their own new journey into hell.

And so these personal and so different adventures are started in all the hearts and minds of those whose door he knocks on. Some receive blessings for their forgiveness, and close the door on him a little lighter of heart, others close the door having invited in a little more darkness than was there before, and started a small but growing battle to emerge from it.

All will emerge, all will find peace and light, but some have a battle ahead.

Including the old man, as he dispenses blessings and curses with his rounds, unwittingly acting as the hand of fate on this dusty day in this dusty town, while his wife waits at home, blithely making a light lunch and preparing for her one last night here before catching their train home next day, unaware of the unwitting baggage her husband is picking up as he trudges round the town, and will have to dispense with once and for all before they can both be free.

Because the decision for change, while a good one if it is change for the better, can only be truly dealt with if the baggage from the old life is also dealt with. No loose ends.

And so deal with it they will. How? Who knows? Not them yet, since they don't know they have it. They think this round of apologies and sucking up the insults and being grateful for the smiles, is it. Ha. Little do they know.

But for now, there is the quiet sense of progress in the right direction – not a mistaken sense, it is as it should be, and even the filth and muck and horror that will be showered on them shortly will be as it should be, though it sure as hell won't feel like it.

How to tell? How to tell the good, cathartic shower of shit hitting you, from the bad, descent-into-fresh-new-hell one?

They'll find out, for sure. It'll become clear as they wade through it, cursing themselves for having taken these steps into what they thought was a good new future. It'll be clear because as they wade through it and it keeps coming thick and fast, they'll still be heading back towards their hearts' desire, and so every now and then a glimpse will be allowed them, just a glimpse mind, of their destination. A brief glint of that distant light, a fleeting smell of the baking bread and cakes on a windowsill that will be theirs soon, as soon as their task is complete, and then the house of flowers and the garden of milk and honey will be theirs to fully inhabit, not just as fleeting visitors.

* * *

At the old home, she prepares lunch. Not much, nothing much in this house and the shops are half empty, but she can make do, and so a repast of broth and old bread re-heated and an egg will do. A glass of water to wash it all down. It's fine. There's so much, back home, and so much better to look forward to, that this meagre offering stands, for her, as a beginning. A small, lean start to an abundant and full future.

She wonders how her girls are doing – are they getting anxious at the thought of the family reunited? Are they doing their chores? Are they arguing amongst themselves and having power struggles in their new-found independence? Probably. They're fine, and they'll be fine. She's only away a day.

As she is pondering how the girls will cope, that is when he returns. Exhausted, and emotionally and spiritually battered from the constant assault at the hands of good and bad vibes, he collapses into a chair and, seeing the less than glorious lunch before him, thanks his wife and wishes fervently for a glass of wine. Futile wish in this house, of course, but there is solace in her presence, and the fact that she has prepared food for him, and even more, the fact that she strokes his head and kisses his old cranium and pats him like a dog, and all seems a little better.

They sit down to their skimpy meal and no sooner is the first spoonful of broth to his lips than there is a knock on the door.

What?

They look at each other, stunned. Maybe, obviously, a delayed response to his outing. The spoons go down, and he levers himself out of his chair and shuffles on tired feet to the door.

There before him stands none other than the angry man, the one whose words brought about this change. He stands, contrite, and offers his own apology for having slammed the door in his face only minutes earlier, and offers apologies to his wife, who he sees with her hands in her lap in front of her cooling broth, and an apology for disturbing their lunch. The old man apologises for there being cause for apology, and all is reconciliation and a burgeoning kindness and relief fills the air like a sudden gust, and suddenly he inside, at their table, sharing a bowl of broth out of new-found, or newly rekindled friendship, not hunger because he's already eaten.

A new lightness fills the no-longer-angry man's body, and laughter bubbles out of him like sparkles in water, and it's infectious, and suddenly the house is reverberating to a sound so long banished from its walls – the sound of fun. A meal shared and enjoyed, and laughter for goodness sake!

A good few hours later, the door to the not-so-gloomy house creaks open to release a now happy man, waved off with smiles and hugs and more laughter, and passing folk try not to stare, and try not to let their mouths hang open in shock to see the old man and his smiling wife wave off their visitor with fond words and promises to do this again soon.

The town is in shock. Not only has the old man been apologising, not only has his wife come back to him, but he's entertaining! And the guest left laughing! They've had fun!

What on earth is going on?

Many puzzle and chuckle at the oddness of it. Many feel a bit lighter now this old gloom seems ready to disperse. But some feel rattled by the change. Some were settled into their old grudge, the comfortable knowledge that there was the enemy, the old bugger, someone they could comfortably and with routine familiarity, complain about and curse and blame for whatever needed it. Now, if he's choosing to shift and change and release himself of his gloom and meanness, where does that leave everyone else? How can you complain and moan and blame someone who sees guests off happy and laughing and with hugs?

They'll put a stop to this. They'll get to the bottom of it. Something's up, not right, not as it should be. There's trickery afoot for sure, they think and whisper. And they'll get to the bottom of it.

* * *

And so, the little grey town continues its day of surprises and reconciliations and new found friendship and new found anger and suspicion and whispering, each inhabitant alone, for now, in their thoughts and surprise. Soon the thoughts will be shared and new alliances forged and old friendships ruptured, all over the simple choice of whether to forgive or not.

The old man and his wife will go on their way, on to their new life, unaware of the new battle lines being drawn, the campaigns being mounted, and the siege to come, as they set off lighter of heart and step to what they believe will be an easy glide into old age.

And it will, ultimately, they just have to get past the weirdness first, past the old festering anger and the desire to make him pay, and the reluctance to let go of old sores, old familiar pains that feel like they define their owner. Without them, what would they be? Would they even continue to be? These long-held grudges are like life-blood to some and, suddenly robbed of them, of the need to hold onto them, they feel empty, lost, undefined. So they fight for them, for their continuance, for their right to life. Much loved and nurtured, they want to see them thrive, their babies, not be hacked down with no warning and nothing to take their place.

This is the battle they face, a struggle to separate parent from child, grudge from grudge holder, and it's never an easy one.

But at least now they have each other again, the old man and his old wife. Took a lifetime to come about, but come it did and now it's here, this reconnection, and they're going to keep it happy and shiny and good till the end.

This will be their armoury, this new confidence in their ability to be together. This will keep them strong in the face of assaults and insults and a new and bitter war waged on their union. This will be their salvation. If they can hold strong.

14

"We are here today gathered, to learn from our mistakes. We are here today having all, at some point in our lives, made mistakes. Big ones, small ones, significant, life-changing mistakes, and insignificant, fleeting ones that affected little. But all serve a purpose. All are a lesson. Do you hear, children?"

A chorus of "Yes" echoes around the place. An especially loud one from the back – a small ginger haired child, unusual in these parts, so he stands out. He has made a mistake, just yesterday. He caught his hands in the latch of the gate while letting the cows out – both hands in there, why? No idea. But it hurt. And now he knows not to be so stupid again. Open the latch the way he was shown by his father and not like an idiot and he won't have sore thumbs to show for it. Lesson learnt.

Another child remembers that he only ever told the truth when it suited him. He enjoyed making things up and watching people's baffled faces when he came up with tales and explanations that sounded good but didn't quite tally with what they knew. He enjoyed his feeling of superiority as they battled, unbeknownst to him, with deciding whether he was a little slow in the head, or crazy and really believed the things he said, or a downright liar. They battled with decisions of whether to pity or dislike him, and that made them wary of him, and when it was decided that probably he was a liar, he was then largely shunned, in a polite and courteous way, but no longer included in conversations or asked many questions, because they knew the fabrications that would come out.

He found out how they saw him the hard way, sadly for him. He had a tale to tell, a true tale, and it was a good one, a fabulously interesting one, and he was going to be the hub of the town's interest and focus for being the bearer of it. But like the boy who cried wolf, when he told his this-time-true tale of wonder, all scoffed and dismissed him, and mocked "yes, yes, of course it happened" and his tale of splendid magic and surreal beauty that had so moved and inspired him, was met with chuckles and laughter and a belittling knuckling on the head.

His tale of wonder was his lesson. His one true chance to shine, honestly and with splendour, was treated as yet another of his tall tales, and instead of propelling him to local fame, served as a lesson, a strong and now well ingrained one, to learn from his mistakes and see that if he wanted to be believed from now, to never tell another lie. Harsh lesson for a child so young, but a good one.

So, sermon done, have all learnt a little something? Most have. Some have simply dozed through it as always, and come away a little wiser since their sleep, as always, has lowered their barriers and allowed the priestly wisdom to creep into their being unchallenged, and so they leave feeling good and virtuous and with an unconscious lesson floating unnoticed in their mind, and their unconscious response to it bubbling up happily and filling their being just in time for lunch.

But for some, one in particular, the lesson has not been learnt. One who holds onto his mistakes and sees them as justified. They are his and they are going to stay till he's done with them.

He has come visiting, visiting family long unseen, and come on a mission. He has found out where the old man's wife fled to, and where the old man plans to make his home, and has come to make trouble.

It is a beautiful day, but inside this visitor's heart the day is heavy with mischief. He has not forgotten the anger and grief caused him when the old man ended their friendship and that of their families. He was happy and their families were happy with their long and easy friendship, and when the misery came and took the old man, all changed for them all.

The visitor has not forgotten his wife's sadness at losing her confidante, nor his children's tantrums and tears at no longer being allowed to play with their young playmates. He pitied those poor girls and the poor wife, increasingly shut up in that dark house, shut off from the life and pulse of the town and of existence itself, but rage was his overwhelming emotion, rage at how his family suffered, he thought. In reality, the truth he kept from himself, the lie his body absorbed and wouldn't release so he could never allow himself to grieve over it, was that the rage was over his loss. He was bereaved, bereft, of his close, closest, friend and ally, lost to him when all fell dark around the old man, and he has never been able to forgive that theft of friendship, companionship, heart-to-heart closeness that he and the old man shared in their youth and young adulthood. The loss cut him and burnt his soul till he too was filled up with an empty longing that could never be filled or made good again.

He feels righteous now. He wants to ensure others don't get fooled like he was. He's come to tell his long-unvisited family a few truths about their new neighbour, "for their own good," he tells himself.

'For their own good' – that lethal phrase. Always used when something unkind or unpleasant is about to be perpetrated on some unwitting soul. Maybe it is sometimes 'for their own good' but more often than not, it should be "for my own good" or "because you deserve punishment and it'll make me feel good to do it." Isn't that so?

He doesn't think so. Thinks that's nonsense. So he sits in his happy family reunion and sips his cool aperitif in the fresh shade from the hot sun, and plans how he will broach the subject.

Pretty easily actually. The new arrivals are on everyone's tongue. The prettiness of the girls and the strangeness of the man and how the woman couldn't wait to get shot of him.

So the tale of the wife doing the rounds of apology with the old man is of great curiosity and interest to all gathered.

Far from sharing in the angry repulsion the visitor feels for this deed, they are agog, and feel compassion and heart-warmth at the tale. Not the intended reaction at all.

So he has to go deeper to get them to see it his way, for their own good, so they don't get burnt by the old man and his devious, treacherous friendship.

He tells of their old friendship betrayed, of his own kind heart lacerated, of his family bereft. The family listen and commiserate, but rejoice that the old man is so changed. This isn't working at all.

The visitor has had enough. He tells them they are fools if they allow themselves to be blinded by his newly civil attitude. He tells them he has no time for those whose eyes are closed to the truth. He drinks up his aperitif (too good to leave) and marches out of the house, dignity held high (he hopes) and leaves before lunch.

15

Do you believe in hell? He does, the new visitor to the town of baking and happy children and welcoming Station Master's wife. He is going through it now in his anger at seeing this happy town that bears the weight of the old man's new habitation so easily.

Why him? Why does he have it so easy after causing so much misery? The visitor never stopped to think, to ponder, what might have happened to change his friend. He just saw the effect on himself and felt blame. He never thought how it might be for his old friend – did he suffer? Did he feel the change and battle against it? Was there a war raging inside his mind? Had his soul become a battlefield of forces beyond himself? How did it start? Could it have an end?

All these questions went unasked in the visitor's pain and blame, and so he never tried to help, although he did make a small attempt to understand initially, so he could have some explanation to give his children. But he didn't delve. So the questions were mute and, naturally, answers could never present themselves.

He just carried the anger with him. Even after so many years, when all had become accustomed to the change and it was now as if it had always been, it clearly lay dormant, since it has now resurfaced with such fervour.

He wanders the streets now in the midday sun, having walked out on his hosts because they wouldn't see things his way, and wonders what to do. Where to go? He could go back home – he has his own transport, lucky man – or he could stay and continue with his mission of mischief and malice, although he would die if he could see that's what it is. He thinks he's doing the right thing. Can't see that anything that causes pain, digs up old dirt, rehashes the past, without an ultimate goal of making it right, can never be good.

He wants revenge. Pure and simple. Sees it as his right. Is prepared to move from his recent happy state, backwards into old anger and blame, for revenge. A bit pathetic, but his to overcome. His personal battle and testing ground, and maybe some good will come of it. Maybe it will clear the old blockages and he will come through it a better, more open and loving person.

We'll see.

* * *

Meanwhile, the old man and his old wife pack up their old house and, to their surprise, find themselves saying goodbye to old friends as they make their way to the train.

At the station, more friends are there to see them off – some out of curiosity, to see if the change they witnessed at their door was real, some to make sure they get on the train, others simply to reconnect once more, joyous in the passing of an old feud and the rekindling of an old friendship.

So, for whatever reasons they have come, there is a farewell party at the station.

Gifts are handed over – biscuits and cordial for the journey, a little bauble for the girls, a hug and a kiss for the wife from an old, lost friend. All is jovial and warm and the air is filled with a kindness the town hasn't seen for a while. And in it all, the station gleams a little whiter and the flowers seem to bloom a little brighter so that everyone comments on how clear the light is today, how clean everything looks, as though there has been a shower of rain.

And so the train comes, and the couple get on to waves and kisses and hugs and fond farewells and invitations, genuine and meant, to come and visit their new home.

And then the metal monster is moving on, clanging and whistling and howling its departure, and all wave and shout out their goodbyes, and smiles are everywhere, lighting up the day even more.

The old man and the old wife sit back in their seats as the last waving hand fades from sight, and smile, astonished, and gaze at each other in a silence that speaks volumes of how surprised they are. A small miracle has happened. It is, to them, as though all the darkness of the past decades has been blown away, dispersed in the air as if made of dust, so easily gone for something that seemed to have such weight.

Their lightness fills them and bubbles up, sparkling, into laughter, gales of happy, joyous laughter that fills the carriage and the train so that other passengers think there must be some very amusing stories being told back there.

Enjoy it, old folk, because it'll be a while before this merriment returns.

* * *

He comes to the station, not knowing what to do with himself, and sits at the station bar, propping his chin in his hand and elbow on the marble counter. His mind whirls but his body is immobile. As is the bar tender in front of him, waiting for his order.

The visitor jolts to consciousness again, "um"s and "ah"s, and orders a coffee. Must keep a clear head. A plan. What to do?

Coffee comes, thick, black, and he sweetens it and sweetens it again – if only the sugar would work its way to his heart and sweeten that, then things might take a turn for the better. But it won't take that route, and things will take the route that has been decreed by his soul, overflowing with bile.

He is drinking his second coffee, even thicker and sweeter, as the bells start their clanging, heralding the train's arrival.

He watches it pull in, metal screeching on metal, and huff and puff of brakes, and the whole thing coming to a shuddering and epic stop in front of him.

And there, amongst the descending passengers, he spots him. The old enemy, his captive wife, laughing, both of them, big stupid grins on their evil faces, and his rage surges upwards and erupts out of his mouth like a boil popping.

He roars his displeasure and years of hurt and betrayal, so that the bar tender whips his little coffee cup away, fearing for its safety, and hurries round to the far side of the bar to hustle this crazy person out.

But the visitor has got a lead on him and has propelled himself outside all by himself, and is charging, head down like a bull, at the old man.

Crowds part in astonishment at his onslaught, scattering children and luggage and hats and parcels like a giant hand has come down amongst them and ruffled them all.

He charges on towards the old man, whose smile is now frozen on his face as he watches this crazy person bulldoze his way across the tracks, through the crowds, towards him. His wife, similarly frozen, snaps to suddenly, and as the crazy visitor's head is about to make contact with her husband's chest, she shoves the old man out of the way.

So the visitor misses his mark and instead charges, full pelt, into the wife. Into her side, cracking ribs, sending her sprawling across the rails, and banging her head hard on the edge of the platform.

Having made contact, the visitor raises his head and sends out a roar of victory, short lived when he sees who his mark was. The old man scurries over to his wife, who lies motionless across the ground, and sets up a wail that pierces to the quick.

The scattered passengers rush to see what has happened, and in no time a doctor has materialised and is bent over her, and several men have grabbed hold of the visitor and have him pinned into immobility between them. But they needn't worry that he'll flee, because he has just seen the result of his handiwork, the wife, motionless on the ground, and he sets up his own wail, of regret and anger at the harm he has caused the wrong person, and that his intended victim now squats unharmed, physically, only inches from him.

How could he get it so wrong? What on earth compelled him to do that? He was never a violent man, and now this – this taking of a life (is she dead?), this cracking of bones and heads over a stupid withdrawal of friendship.

The blood now seeping from her head has shocked him to his senses and he sees how pathetic his held-onto anger was and how terrible the consequences.

He doesn't notice he is being marched away – he sees only the wife, lifted by many arms and carried off quickly, the old man wailing in her wake, all trace of the earlier laughter wiped from his face so completely it is as if it had never, ever been.

A sad homecoming after such a joyful start.

The girls are told – nobody is sure how the news has travelled so fast, but it is the nature of bad news to travel at lightning speed – and as he is propelled by strong arms towards the town's little police station, the visitor sees the girls running full pelt down the hill towards a house where, simultaneously, their unconscious mother is being carried.

And so, the much anticipated family reunion takes place under circumstances very different to those they had planned.

They meet and hug their estranged father in a torrent of tears, and all stay close, so close, as they crowd into the doctor's house, and stay close as the doctor and nurse carry their mother into an examination room and close the door on them and leave them to thoughts and terrors of the worst, of possibly their last sight of their adored mother with blood on her temple and her ribs sticking out weirdly.

* * *

Unhappy day. Unhappy reunion, but vast the well of love that surges up between them all, including their errant but returned father, and vast the outpouring of it that washes through the cracks in the door separating them from their beloved, and soft and warm the flow of it as it settles in and around the battered old woman lying on the examination bed being tended to and checked for life by the anxious and gifted doctor and his equally gifted nurse.

The surge of love and prayers sent fervently up to the cosmos form a cloud of protective energy that settles around the patient, cocooning and patching and fixing, because of course God is looking down, having heard the rumpus, and having set them all on this helter skelter path of return to him, isn't going to abandon them now.

They've started this journey, so they're going to finish it, so he lets the cloud of love and prayer for life and recovery do its work, and, left to its own devices, it settles around the hands of the nurse and doctor and, coupled with their skills, brings about miraculous recovery.

The head is patched, the bruises treated with ice, the ribs freed from the constraints of the dress, gently manipulated as much as is possible back into some sort of alignment, then the chest bound to keep them there, then prayers said to make it all fix and heal and keep her breathing.

She does breathe, though as she regains consciousness it is jarring and painful enough to prompt her to cry out in agony. This cry provokes a response from outside the door – yelps of delight that she breathes, lives, feels enough to have pain. Happy day!

And so, the unhappy homecoming takes a turn for the better, and becomes the most wonderful of homecomings – she has been returned to them.

Now they will care for her as she has them all these years, and nurse and feed her, and tend her head and ribs, and not speak too loudly, nor make her laugh (too painful to endure, but it won't be hard in these coming days). They will do all to ensure a happy, easy, successful convalescence so she is returned to them as she was, better than she was, because she'll be so rested after all their attentions.

16

They are all there, around her big bed, watching her sleep. Nobody speaks, they barely dare breathe for fear of waking her from her restorative peace.

All stare though, deep into her head and heart and ribs, trying to see the healing take place, willing it to move on faster, unaware that the energy pouring out of their eyes and minds and bodies is like a furnace roaring all around her and rousing her from her slumber.

She stirs, her eyelids move, eyeballs rolling this way and that, and to a chorus of muted gasps and whispers, she wakes. Looks at them all gathered around her like mourners around a coffin, and gasps herself.

"Am I dead?" she squeals.

"No!" they chorus, some shocked, some relieved.

"Then get back, you're suffocating me" she barks, flapping her hands at them all, and they scuttle back like chickens hustled out of their coop. She tries to lever herself up on one elbow and lets out a yelp of pain as the still unhealed and displaced ribs poke her. The girls and the old man all rush in again to save her from her discomfort, and all are levering and pulling and plumping pillows and squawking at each other so that it truly does resemble a chicken run. All it needs now is a pillow to burst and scatter feathers for the transformation to be complete.

Eventually she is settled into a sitting position, and all can breathe and take a step back and be silent for a minute.

There. She looks at them all, her brow furrowed under the bandages, and snaps "Haven't you got chores to do? Do the dishes wash themselves? Do the floors sweep themselves? Who's watering the vegetables? What are you all doing standing around here like cretins?"

A shocked silence reverberates around the room. Mutely, they steal glances at each other to check they heard right, then put the uncharacteristic harshness down to the bump on the head (which it is, and it's going to get much worse – this is only the beginning) and with many gentle and whispered exhortations to "rest" and "sleep" and "relax, we'll do everything now," they back out of the room on tip toes, and shut the door.

Downstairs, family conference. They sit around the kitchen table and discuss their mother's strangeness. One of them has heard that bumps on the head can change a person irreparably, and voicing this thought plunges them all into a pit of gloom and fear that their beloved mother has been lost to them, and a new, harsh, critical, insulting mother given to them in her stead. The irony is not lost on them, especially in the case of the old man, that they have lost one critical and insulting and harsh parent, him, renewed now with love and new life, and gained a new one – him for her, tit for tat, old rope for new rope, and so on.

This prospect is a dreadful one – they are still in such early days of their new and marvellous life, that it seems insanely cruel to have it ripped from them already.

Their fear and belief in the bad that they envision forms a cloud around them, much like their earlier cloud of love and prayer and hope for life, and just as that cloud of good, positive, energy settled around their mother and helped her body begin to heal, so this new cloud of dark, negative energy rises up through the stones of their house, up through the floorboards and the cracks in the walls, and seeps invisibly into her room. There it pools around the feet of the bed, for negative energy doesn't have the buoyancy of the positive, and slowly curls its way up the bed legs, and up the edges of the blankets, onto the sheets, and slip-slides its greasy way onto her skin.

She feels a slight shudder running up her as this wash of gloom coils and twists upwards, and a distinct feeling of bad temper clamps itself onto her temples as it reaches her crown and settles, hat-like, around her head.

Oh boy, she's cross. She sits up in bed, head aching, ribs aching, (the doctor's orders not to laugh – pah, no danger of that in this house of stupid, idle girls) and frets over all the work that is not being done, or worse, being done badly so she'll have to re-do it all as soon as she can get up. Every single last bit of it, no doubt.

She listens for activity down below and, hearing none, assumes none is taking place. Rightly so, since they are all sitting around the kitchen table constructing and increasing the size of this massive cloud of negative gloom and doom, feeding it with their strong and unswerving focus and oh so quickly and with great passion, creating a monster.

It'll take some work to undo what they are creating with so little time and effort. It'll take a lot more time and focus and effort to dismantle it and build in its place a new cloud of love and light and positive thought to help reclaim their mother from the dark prison she is being sucked into as they fret and fuss.

They can't see it, but she is being pulled from them, millimetre by millimetre, into an invisible cage of darkness that holds tight to its victims, doesn't let them go ever, if it has the choice. They have to be prised and pulled and unstuck and chiselled free of its clutches once it's got them.

They don't see this happening, and they certainly don't see their enormous contribution to its happening, with their belief in it. They won't see it till it's too late and she has slipped out of their grasp. Then they'll have a battle on their hands to break her out. Which they will, it is their destiny to be reunited and happy and at peace in their new home. They feel it, know it in their bones, which is why this new detour has taken them so unawares, so unprepared.

They'll come round, rally, see their mistake in feeding the monster, and start their campaign to break her out, but not yet. They have their period in hell to suffer first, their purification, needed to make them clear channels to receive all the bounty that this town, this world, this existence, has to offer. But they have to shed every last vestige of their dark past first, and their mother has more to shed than them. All the years of torment and darkness in the old house, where she endured and endured instead of making the choices to free them all, all those years have stored up great darkness inside her which all has to be released, a massive blockage, like a well and truly bunged up pipe, and this, God decreed, was the most efficient way of rodding that pipe.

So there we have it. Paradise found, then lost again, and now to be found once more in the unknowable (to them) future. Requires hope, blind faith, and positive vibration. If any one of those fails, they slide backwards until it is fired up again and they resume forward momentum.

Tough times. Tough choices. But they are there, and must be dealt with.

Unhappy family. Unhappy house. Sad reunion, that should have been so good, should have been the happy ending they all wanted and felt they deserved.

It's coming, their happy ending, but not yet. Not yet.

17

See? The light shines bright in her room yet they daren't go up and check on her, see if there's anything they can do for her, check she's still breathing, because she'll bite their heads off.

They watch from their position in the garden, watch the illumined glass in the fading daylight, and wonder what to do next, wonder where it all went, their fleeting happiness, wonder how they could have been so blasé about it while it was with them. How could they not have known to appreciate it fully, live every moment to the full (they did, though they've forgotten now), enjoyed every little sip of cordial from their own fruits, drunk around their own garden table under their own flower-laden canopy on their own happy veranda (they did enjoy every bit of it, it simply seems faded now)?

All is tainted in memory by the present change and loss. All is different, and looks, in their current pessimistic view of the world, to be here to stay.

Unhappy changes. Miserable reversal of such blessed fortunes. All sit in their individual, lonely gloom, not sipping their now tainted cordials, watching and listening for a change, but hearing and seeing nothing.

* * *

Nothing is the very opposite of what is going on in the little sick room. The place is in a frenzy of activity – mental, not physical, but busy busy busy nonetheless.

Mother's mind is in a fervour of fretting and worrying and criticising and blame and all manner of negatives. She's astonished she never before noticed what a shocking job the girls made of sweeping and folding and ironing. The creases in the sheets are all wrong and there is a dust ball under the wardrobe. She can see it from here. What were they thinking? Thinking of boys and dresses and dancing no doubt, not of the work they were supposed to be doing.

Too much idleness by far in this place. All this strolling and gardening and having people in for coffee weakens the mind and the resolve and leads to stagnation of the spirit.

As the sad and backwards-looking thoughts charge around her mind, they seem familiar. She remembers them from somewhere, from some other mind and mouth, and they have a nasty, sour taint. Can't put her finger on where, who, when.

In confusion, she bats between what she sees as their clear logic, and the bitter aftertaste they leave, as though they were something she had only recently escaped from. On the other hand, they quieten her anger, this new rage that has bubbled up from God-knows-where inside her, as though something has popped in the deep subterranean mazes of her being, and with the bump on the head, been jolted free to float fast to the surface and escape.

How could she have been unaware of it for so long? It mars all memories of the past and thoughts of the future and allows her no rest, no moment of silence to allow her head to quieten and the heat in her brain and her ribs to cool.

She needs a cool breeze to shut all this boiling rumpus up. So she levers herself out of bed, with much grunting and yelping, and throws open her window.

There, down below, staring up like startled rabbits, her useless family. She glares at them, the bubbling ire in her head coming to a fore at the sight of their asinine faces, then as the evening breeze caresses and mops at her hair and brow, it fizzles and escapes into the twilight, and she can relax a bit.

She sighs. Her face softens as the sigh works on her heart and softens it a little too, and this prompts sighs of relief from down below, and suddenly all are a little calmer, a little soothed, and all can finally, at long last, take a breath.

* * *

Later, night has settled around the town and the surrounding hills and mountains, and the family have settled once more around the kitchen table. Mother included.

All are silent, wary of saying the wrong thing and spoiling the atmosphere of peace (relative) and harmony (sort of). At least there's no shouting or telling off going on, and they'd all like to keep it that way.

The old woman has settled herself into a chair and seems to be pain-free for now, and so is silent. She is looking around her, at jobs done and not done, and a battle is raging inside her head about whether to criticise and scold, or let it slide. It seems to her that since that maniac ran at her, part of his crazy brain has taken up residence inside her own, as if when his head came to a halt against her ribs, his mind kept going, into her skin and muscle and, bouncing off her spine, shot upwards till its progress was stopped in its tracks by her skull.

Momentum arrested, it stayed where it landed and hasn't been able to find a way out since.

She feels the battle of two people, two identities, swarming and invading her privacy, her thoughts, her ideas, every second, and though she has been fervently cleaning out her ears and blowing her nose since she returned to consciousness, it hasn't been enough to clear out an exit path from her head.

She firmly believes she has the crazy visitor's mind in her head. Better that wrong belief, than to know and understand the truth right now – that the crazy visitor simply dislodged what was long buried in her – God's rodding iron – and set her hidden rage and fury on its own path to freedom.

Like a boil, her suppressed emotions need to erupt to freedom, coming through her flesh and blood and making their presence felt all the way until, like infection and pus, they pop through the skin with much pain and discomfort and inflammation of the mind and nerves, and dispel into nothing. Gone. Body left calm, mind calm, as if nothing ever was.

Catharsis. Good, eh?

Not so good while it's happening though. Not so good for all, right now, as the infection in their wife and mother's being creeps closer to the surface in its flight to freedom.

The silence around the table has gone on long enough. Her logical mind has fought a good fight this evening, trying and succeeding, till now, in keeping the peace. But enough is enough.

"Oh for goodness sake, what is the matter with you bunch of moronic fools, all staring at the wall and your feet and each other as though you'd find nuggets of wisdom there. Find a broom, find a dish cloth. Find the damned dust balls under every bit of furniture in this damned house. Are you all blind? Or do you simply enjoy living like pigs, troughing down on your own filth? One day I take my eye off you all, and you revert to type – idle, good-for-nothing, useless, stupid girls. Good luck to you all if you think you'll find anyone fool enough to marry you. Good luck to me if I think I'll ever get shot of any of you. Thought I'd got shot of him and now look. Back like a dog with his tail between his legs."

Silence. A lip quivers here, a sniff there, a shuffle as the old man quietly shifts his chair back and, trying to make as little noise as possible so as not to draw attention to himself, he creeps towards the back door with the intention of removing himself to the sanctuary of his wood shed. Not so fast.

"And what do you think you're doing? Don't you think it's about time you did some work around the house? A life-time of slaving for you is quite enough. Now it's your turn." And with that she gets up, maybe intent on showing the nervous old man what his new chores are to be, but the movement is too much at this early stage in her convalescence, and a rib digs in, and she yelps, and it digs in a bit more, and mercifully causes her enough pain to prompt her to choose a return to bed rather than showing her family what for.

So they all troop up the stairs behind her, no-one daring to help so as not to incur a volley of abuse, and she hauls herself back into bed and, with much muttering and complaining and belittling, settles in for the night.

Phew. Thank the Lord that's over.

"My pleasure" says the Lord, still watching and monitoring progress of the rising infection/pus popping/boil lancing situation. He sees all is taking its proper time, progress is as it should be, and he's pleased.

They're not, needless to point out. They see nothing but dark days ahead, and though if they stay positive and hopeful all will indeed turn out as it should, it is going to be hard to maintain a positive outlook. Any slide into gloom, any detour, and subsequent decision that it is all too much and is never going to get better, any loss of hope or focus on recovery, could and will change their path to success.

This is their potential stumbling block. They must keep their eyes looking up, heads up to sky not down to the depths, for what you focus on is what you get, remember?

Hope begets hope begets success. Gloom begets more gloom begets utter despondence and hopelessness and a slow sure slide into hell. And that's a hard place to get out of. Requires all the hope and dedication and positive thinking that was lacking in the first place, doubled. Big job. Hard task. Best to catch it early and not allow the slide to go full stretch – much easier to arrest in its early stages.

But it's easier to judge the state and progress of others than it is our own, so though God watches and smiles, he can't choose their next step for them, can't choose how long it'll take for them to reach their goal. He knows they'll reach it, for all do ultimately, but they, as all, will choose how long it takes to get there and how smooth or rough their path will be. All choices, see?

Back to that. It always comes back to that. Make your choices and make them good ones, for your life, the quality and nature of it, depends on them.

18

Are you ready? Ready for change and movement and slip sliding of new and greasy change, slithering here and there and everywhere but where you choose? They're not.

They lie awake in their beds, staring into blank night, and wonder at what dark awfulness tomorrow will bring in this dreadful new detour their life has taken.

The old man, in the safety of the wood shed, contemplates his new surroundings which should have held such hope and new-found peace and harmony, and hears only his now demented wife's babblings and criticisms and ire, and sees in them his own ragings that welled up inside him like an unstoppable eruption for so many years.

He knows, sees, now, what it must have been like for them all, living with him in that state. He has had one day of losing his wife to the rage, and feels a depth of despair he never imagined possible. They must have had that on a daily basis for years and decades, never seeing an end to it, just day after grey day of rage and fear of speaking and trepidation about the reaction any one of their actions could provoke.

His remorse threatens to overwhelm him, and is held in check only by his bewilderment and grief that it should now have taken over his much loved wife.

He has the time and inclination and will now to make amends to them all, and will try somehow to make it better for his suffering wife. He doesn't know how yet, because he doesn't understand how his darkness suddenly left him, (we do – this town made it leave) but he will work hard to fix her and make her good again as he has been made good. He'll do what she asks, to keep the rage down, and constantly think and examine the recesses of his brain to find what triggered his cure.

They made vows, him and her, they loved each other, love each other still, and although their marriage has mostly been the 'in sickness' part of their early promise to each other, and largely the 'for worse' part too, he aims to lead them into the 'in health' and 'for better' parts, that their twilight years can glow with the goodness and riches they should have been showered with throughout their tainted lives.

* * *

While he thinks and chews things over, so does she. Her head hurts, throbs, and the two people in there don't seem to want to sleep. The old her is in terrible pain over the way the new her is treating everyone. She sees the new her repeating the patterns and behaviours of the old man all those years, behaviour that led them all to leave him and come here to this sunny place. The old her is now aching with fear that, seeing the new her inheriting all the old, despised traits of their past, they will up and leave her just as they left him. She will be abandoned in her strange new prison of wretched duality and broken bones, and they will maybe return to the old grey house, because she will be here, and then all will be unhappy.

This sunny, scented house will be a poor place to be without her loved ones, but the wretched crazy in her head is doing its best to drive them out. It's there now, listening to all that old-her is thinking, and no doubt plotting some new outrage to vomit out of her mouth when she next sees her family.

Poor, wretched woman. She has no idea that this infected monstrosity that lives now in her head is her own buried self. No idea that its evolution from suppression to expression is a necessary step to her salvation and freedom. All she sees is its potential to drive her family away, make them hate her like they hated the old man, and that would break her heart, shatter it, destroy it and her completely, with no hope of recovery.

And so the night wears on, a long, weary night of sleeplessness and toiling minds and worry and fretting and a general undercurrent of utter misery, made sharper by contrast with their so recent happiness.

Unhappy family. Sad rooms, sighing with loneliness and a void where love and unity so recently were.

It'll take a lot more than a series of heart massaging sighs to get this lot up and about and happy again. It is their time for gloom. They will emerge again, because all of life on this earth, in these fleshy incarnations, is contrast. Constant contrast, ups and downs, goods and bads, lights and darks, sweet and sour, hard and soft; through these we learn and experience, and through learning, grow, and through growth, come to make better choices next time, in years to come, in lives to come.

They are seeing their contrasts now. Not that they haven't seen this one before, but they see it better now they have had a taste of the sweet to their sour, so hopefully now they are equipped to do something to make it better, choose a return to the sweet, the soft, the scented. They may have to work hard to put those new choices into practice, but no doubt there will be lessons along the way that will give them more learning, more understanding, more experience, on which to base better choosing.

Ah well. On and on, choose this, choose that, can't someone else do it? Can't they just have peace for once? That thought fills all their minds, but they are so close to having their peace, they simply have to hold on, deal with this last hurdle, and they should be on the home stretch, if all goes well. But of course they can't see that – they are here to learn and experience, not to be led. So they have to battle on, so close to ultimate success and yet so unaware of it.

Cruel, really, isn't it? Yes and no. Harsh not to be allowed to rest and enjoy the end of the journey to their goal of happiness, but so much more valuable to experience the lessons of that journey.

"Yes, sure, easy to say when you're not living it" they think.

And so it goes. Learning versus peace and ease; contrast again.

Choices, contrast, why can't we all just sit under our canopies of lilac and wisteria and drink a cool aperitif and enjoy life?

Their cool veranda glows soft in the moonlight.

She's lying above that veranda, the scent of flowers filling her room and her nose, and it has a soothing effect on her. The pure, simple scent of flowers that can do no wrong, can make no mistakes or talk nonsense, clears a path in her mind to her heart, and in that scented gap between thoughts, a choice is made. A good choice.

She will watch and see what 'new her' does and thinks and wants to say and says, and try to understand it. 'Old her' will try to nurture and care for it like she has all her girls when they were young and difficult and troubled by their sad life; she will see how she can help it be free of rage, and not judge it. She sees it now as a separate thing from her true self, and with that realisation comes hope, that she can negotiate and communicate with it, come to an understanding with it, and maybe, possibly, hopefully, ultimately either cure and calm it, or get it to leave.

Suddenly the night seems lighter, the moonlight in her room clearer, and the scent of the flowers everywhere.

In their morose semi-sleep, the others feel it too. A light breeze fanning perfume into their hair and sheets, and cooling their overheated imaginings and fears. It lulls them with its sense of new hope and possible solutions, and all fall easily into a deeper, restorative sleep.

Their dreams now will be of how things so recently were, and how they will be again, so they will all wake with untainted memories of happiness and hopes and plans for its restoration to them.

Ah. Calmer night now. Restful, the slumber that finally settles over this embattled family. Peaceful, the dreams they now frolic in. Scented, the air, with hope and new beginnings. About time. Goodnight to them all.

19

Here they all are now, sitting around the kitchen table once more, an uneasy peace fizzing between them. All are polite, excessively so, for fear of whatever might come out of her mouth when she appears, and all chores and tasks are done to perfection and checked and re-checked before she sets foot outside her room. The house shines. It would squeak if anyone ran a finger over any surface, which she might well do.

Not much breathing going on – too tense – so not much blood making its way to their brains, so the stage is set for some bad choices to be made. And, on cue, one of them says something, another snaps without thinking, and suddenly there is a full scale row going on, in hushed tones.

Upstairs, mother/wife sits up in her bed, mind boiling with bitter comments and harsh realities she longs to slap them with. She hears the hissing and sniping, so uncharacteristic, coming from downstairs, and adds another complaint to her long litany.

That's when old-her kicks in, wakes up, shakes itself from scented sleep. Old-her recognises instantly that she is the cause of the disturbance, that new-her has rattled them all and shaken up their peaceful demeanour like a stirrer in a butter churn.

Old-her wants their happy life back and longs to go down and make peace flow amongst them again, as was her role for so many years, but new-her is bubbling ever higher in her being, the pus and infection rising closer and closer to the skin, and is too strong now to overcome.

So old-her does what she decided to do last night, amongst the soothing and mind-clearing scent of flowers, and she will observe. See how it behaves and the choices it makes and try to understand.

Hup – she's out of bed, yelps, clutches her ribs, mutters and curses under her breath (very unlike her), gathers her dressing gown around her, and hobbles and shuffles off downstairs to sort them out.

Obviously new-her is fearless in the face of physical pain. Impressive.

She shuffles down the stairs, and a sudden and total silence falls on the place. Her slippered footsteps clang like pots rattling in the echoing void.

She emerges into the kitchen to a scene of domestic harmony and industry – every one of them, including her aged husband, is doing something, some household chore that seems complete but that they are still working on, so that if she complains it has not been done well, possibly they will claim not to have finished it yet.

Old-her observes their wiliness in the presence of new-her, and recognises they have shifted their behaviour to accommodate this new version of Mother. She observes new-her induces manipulative/deceptive behaviour in them. Interesting.

Old-her weeps, deep down where it's barely heard, to see how she has brought about this unhappy change in her beloved family, but equally deep is the whispered reassurance that when she returns, all will be as it was, their true selves will come out of hiding again and be able to be open and true.

Everything stops as she takes her first step into the kitchen and looks around her. She looks at the chores they are completing and nods her head in approval – good job. There is a miniscule out-breath of relief somewhere in the room, but when she glances up to see where it came from, all are smiling politely at her and inviting her to sit and offering her bread and jam and tea and coffee and whatever else her heart might call out for.

Old-her wants to hug them all and tell them all will be ok and that she loves them more than ever for the hell they are enduring at her hands, but she doesn't. New-her.

She sits and sips tea and nibbles at fresh bread and jam and tries, at least, to stay silent.

The family joins her, trying to maintain the façade of normality, and sip and nibble along with her, although appetites are virtually non-existent and their thirst is unquenchable – their thirst for normality, true normality. How distant it seems, even though they last lived it only yesterday. Breakfast yesterday morning was normal, wasn't it?

And in their mourning of what was, and grief at their sudden loss, they experience a fleeting collective memory – of the scent of the canopy of flowers outside, and the hope and promise of a return to their old lives carried on it.

So the tentative sipping and nibbling glide invisibly into genuine calm over a relatively normal breakfast, with all breathing easily now so the blood can flow unhindered to their brains and set them up for a day of clarity and a sound basis for the taking of good decisions.

And as the normality seeps and creeps around that table with the scent of flowers imperceptibly carried in on the faint summer breeze, a sigh of relief comes out of someone's mouth, then another, disguised here as a lip-smacking, yum-that-was-good sigh of contentment at a gulp of tea, or bite of bread, and there as a settling back in contentedness at a full stomach.

In reality all are sighing with relief that this day has started so well in comparison to how the last one ended.

And, of course, the sighs are infectious; even Mother lets one slip, and so all their hearts benefit from the gentle vibrations in their chest, and all are gently caressed and soothed and set up for a good start to a day of progress towards their ultimate goal.

That's not to say it will be an easy day – too soon for that – but at least they face it with a positive heart and mind, and that will make all the difference.

Aah – happy, easy sound, gentle massage, deep penetrating vibration that touches the soul and opens the channels to the sky and beyond, and on to the angels and guides who look down on them with love and hope, ready with guidance the minute any one of them asks, and on to God who watches, as always, and waits to see what they will do next, and chuckles in anticipation of the day's events to come, in the knowledge that it moves them on, closer to him and to home and to their ultimate happiness, and the knowledge also that they will curse and spit and rebel and kick against all the harsh lessons that are to come, and the knowledge of how they will laugh at themselves when it is all over and they have the leisure to look back at the journey taken, and all the lessons they misunderstood and side stepped, not knowing at the time that there is no side stepping in this course of evolution they have chosen, that a lesson by-passed is a lesson they'll have to return to in this life or the next or the one after that, and so on until their schooling is complete, graduation accomplished, hats thrown in the air in celebration, and ascension gained to the carnival of delights on the other side.

20

See? She's there now, waiting at the gate for him, smiling, wearing her best dress which he loves so much, though he never thought to tell her when she would have appreciated the compliment. So much he never thought to do in his life wasted in misery, and now so many regrets that it might be too late, that she has left behind the person who would have smiled at compliments and laughed at being teased. Such a waste.

* * *

He looks out at his new domicile, the green, the colour, the abundance, and sitting on his little stool outside the wood shed, he counts his blessings.

First time he's done that since – can't remember a time, ever. And what a strange time to start, when his beloved wife has been swallowed up by a stranger who now lives in her mind and he can't make contact, daren't make contact.

Odd time to start, but any time is a good time for appreciation. He appreciates and gives thanks for his little stool, placed outside the wood shed for him to sit and enjoy the summer without bothering them. Blessing no.1. Blessing no.2 – the summer abundance all around him, verdant, bursting with bloom and fruit and scents and the sound of bees and the flash of butterfly wings – glorious. Blessing no.3 – his girls, and his reunion with them. Though he sleeps in the shed (blessing no.4), he eats with them around their blessed (no.5) kitchen table and savours a flavour of how things might have been, had he not spoilt everything.

And on and on, the blue sky, the honey he's eating for breakfast – the one meal he's taking on his own, in his own little space (another), and with each new blessing he recognises, and silently, unknowingly, gives thanks for, the thing appreciated glows a little brighter, as if in thanks for his thanks, and in return he glows a little brighter, and so the blessings and the thanks bounce back and forth between them until he feels joy rising physically in his body from his feet up, like a fizzing current of excitement, prompting him to breathe deeper to feel it better, and with each deeper inhalation it travels faster up his body and intensifies its charge, till he's overflowing with this wonderful sensation of delight and pleasure and appreciation of each and every thing around him.

And the more he appreciates, the more he sees to appreciate, till it seems to him the world is crammed full of such wonders, he can't understand how he could have missed them all these years.

Because he wasn't looking for them, that's how. Simple really. You look for something, sooner or later you find it. There. Question answered.

That seems too simple to him. A huge chunk of his life missing – surely a much more complex and tortuous explanation is required? Nope. He just wasn't looking. For the good, that is. He found what he was searching for at the time though, found it in abundance, just like now he is finding an abundance of beauty and natural miracles all around him. Before, he searched out misery and evil and gloom and idleness and stupidity in every person and every situation, and voilà – the universe delivered. He was surrounded by what he looked for. Works every time. Not always recognised, or appreciated (word of the day, see?) for what it is, but nevertheless, there it is. Delivered as ordered.

Orders are a tricky, sly thing though – "need to watch out for them" he'd think if he could rationalise what was happening to him. You could be ordering away like billy-oh and not realise you're doing it. Look at him – focussing on his family's idleness and gloom and misery – delivered as ordered. Now, focusing for a while on how lovely everything is here and how he loved and missed his family and wanted them back – delivered as ordered.

Have to watch out then, not to focus too much on his wife's craziness, or on getting gout from all this good food he's eating, or on finding it an increasing struggle to walk up hills, especially now he's living up a hill. Better think about gliding up that hill like a butterfly, and it'll come to him.

That's it – that last one – "Stupid," he thinks, "plain stupid," then catches himself. In a quandary now. He's seen how things he thinks about and wishes for are materialising around him, and it is such a relief, and such a pleasure, that he's scared of losing it all, especially now his wife's gone mad – so he wants to keep his focus positive, because he's seeing the results, but he can't help fear creeping in, fear of losing it all.

Before, he'd have made losing it all a reality in his mind, so if and when it happened, the shock would be less and the awfulness of it diminished through invented familiarity. Now he wonders if he made the losses happen. Dilemma! An old habit, a comfortable one, turns out to be a bad one, and he doesn't know what to do now, how to feel comfortable and make himself feel better with all the turmoil that's going on in this family.

Luckily, this train of thought, spiralling into a spiders-web tangle of mind confusion, is interrupted by a shrill shriek.

He shoots from his stool, and head turns this way and that as he tries to re-focus from internal world to external, and it makes him light-headed and he almost falls over.

Again – shriek – from the house (where else?) and he's off. Legs move faster than they have in a long while (so much for fretting about walking uphill) and he's sprinting (ish) across the garden and in through the back door and up the stairs, where the sound came from, and in through a bedroom door, to find one of his daughters, the eldest, lying across her bed with a gash across her forehead.

"What on earth has happened?" he barks to his other girls, all standing around staring, while he hurries to his maimed daughter's side and checks her pulse – beating – and breath – breathing – but she too is unconscious.

"What on earth is happening?" he yells at nobody in particular, at the girls who are mute with horror at the sight of another family member with blood coming out of her head.

No-one has a reply. They found her like this, it seems, and the shrieks were the response of successive girls coming in and finding her like that.

179

They are despatched for water and cloths and towels and the doctor, and between them they manoeuvre the eldest onto the bed and shove pillows under her head, to which she says "ow" – blessed sound – and all rejoice that she lives, and the room is full of the sounds of crying and laughter which brings the youngest, who was despatched to get the doctor, bolting back up the stairs believing her beloved sister has died, and finds herself yelled at to get down to town and get the doctor for goodness sake and stop messing about, and all is concern and relief and tears and questions till the eldest barks out that can she have some peace and quiet please, because her head hurts.

That shuts them up. Quietly, as he dabs a damp cloth at her head, not achieving much other than making her wince, the old man asks, for a third time, "What happened?"

Silence falls like a pall over the room as all eyes turn to her, wide, eager to hear, anxious in case they don't like the reply, and they won't, but she isn't saying anything. Yet.

She chews her lips, and gingerly brushes her fingertips over her wound, and winces, and chews her lips some more.

While all wait.

Finally, eyes rolling to heaven in a mute appeal for help, or understanding, or to just get them to stop staring, she takes a deep breath and prepares to speak.

They lean in.

And a heavy out-breath and a shake of the head. She can't do it.

They lean out again, huffing and telling her to just spit it out.

Another deep breath in, and out it comes, her story.

Mother. Of course. Who else? Their much adored and idolised mother, who has been abducted by the new crazy woman. She didn't like her breakfast in bed, it seems, so after five minutes which must have been spent pondering and tasting it, because it was largely gone when she came in and threw it at her eldest, she came in and threw it at her eldest.

Some part of it, coffee bowl or bread plate, smacked her on the head and shattered – "It's over there under the table" she points out – and indeed it is, minutely blood spattered.

A nasty business. Insults and shouting are one thing, physical violence quite another. Unacceptable. That has never been part of their family life, however dark the bad times were, and it's not going to be now. So decides the old man.

And on that thought, he picks up the blood spattered broken china, delicately, as though the blood it held could somehow be returned to its

181

rightful owner, and with a gentle, so gentle kiss to the throbbing forehead of his eldest, he leaves.

Leaves one sick room and enters another.

And there she is. Sitting up in bed as though nothing was amiss, scowling at him as though *he* had just put a gash in their child's face.

He looks at her. She looks back. He holds out the piece of china. She glances at it and new-her says "pah", and old-her crumples with despair and pain at what she has become and seems to be unable to un-become.

Outside she scowls at him again, unmoved; inside she wails her utter misery to the heavens and beyond and the angels gather to see what causes such unrestrained grief, and they cluster round to hug and reassure her, but it goes unfelt, unnoticed, in the overwhelming, searing agony of that little bloody piece of evidence, that she has hurt her child.

Unhappy day. Doubly unhappy father. Eternally and infinitely devastated mother who cannot climb out of the pit she has fallen into, can see the rim of it, see daylight far above, but can do nothing to get herself back up there.

All seems lost to her, life has vanished from her grasp and a devilish existence has taken its place, too potent and malicious and angry to triumph over.

But there in front of her, that small piece of china with the blood spots, that's all she needs to start her climb out of there.

Buried far beneath her suppressed (or not so suppressed these days) rage, spreading tentacles further than any unexpressed anger at herself and her husband, is her mother-love. She won't have anyone, anyone, attack her children. Especially not some evil crazy version of her that has erupted out of the tenebrous depths of her own hell. It can go right back there and get out of her life and get away and stay away from her children.

The old man still stands in front of her, arm held out clutching the evidence, for her mind-battle has taken place in the blink of an eye, and he marvels at the sight of so much story and emotion and decision-making hurtling across her face.

He is witnessing the birth of the change within her, the new-her losing its superior standing, losing its footing as supreme being inside her head, and as old-her starts her climb up the pit, digging finger nails into the greasy walls for purchase and hauling herself up on nothing but skin, bones and will, he sees glimpses of his beloved in her eyes.

It's the first time since his dreadful return here that he's seen she still lives, and it overwhelms him.

He drops the china and shuffles over to her bed. Even though new-her is still hanging on to residency in her face, he's seen old-her flicker in her eyes, and that's the woman he now puts his arms around. New-her fights him off, pushing and shoving, but for once she is mute – old-her has cut off her vocal chords – and so the old man persists, clamping his arms around her hard, pressing his heart unwittingly against hers, and holds her there, pouring love and appreciation for her survival out through his heart and in through hers, so that with every breath he is filling up with the wonderful fizzing again, and as he overflows with it, it starts to trickle into her, into her heart, and from there, with every valve contraction and every spurt of arterial blood into her flesh and muscle, it spreads.

His love, virus-like, floods her system, and from her dark pit she sees it, lighting up the shiny surface she has to grapple with, and showing her hand holds, foot holds, tiny, miniscule, but there for her to reach for, grab onto, push off from for the next one.

And slowly, painfully, perilously, she edges back towards daylight, towards sanity, towards her old self while the new self slides downwards, missing the holds, gliding back into the pit it came from.

* * *

It's not going to be that straightforward of course. Her return to health will be gradual, and new, or not-so-new-anymore-her, will occasionally shout out from the pit and be heard and be vile, but as old-her gets ever closer to freedom, she is increasingly good at knocking a rock down onto her enemy and shutting her up.

Back on track, although some (God) would say they were never off track, as he watches and nods, hands resting happily on stomach in satisfaction at how their path progresses. Back on track to the their happy ending. Hurrah!

21

He comes to her now, at the gate, every morning before he wakes. She's standing there waiting for him, in her best dress, and now he compliments her. She's young, he's young, they are as they were, and all is beautiful and light and breezy and the world is full of pleasure and delight at their new-found paradise in each other.

That's when he wakes, every morning, having found and complimented his pretty wife in her best dress, and all has the savour of perfection about it.

As does the waking world, with his daughter's cracked head healing and his old wife gradually re-emerging from her private hell, and the new crazy wife slowly diminishing and becoming fainter each day.

The house, the girls, the town, seems lighter for their joy and relief at how things are resolving themselves, and their life coming back to how it should be. The only fly in the ointment is this – crazy visitor, still in the town jail, because he refuses to leave.

Hugely penitent for the damage he caused in his day of blind rage, he now feels irreparably damaged by it. In spite of being told, repeatedly, that the old woman, his ancient friend, is recovering nicely and the damage to her head is waning hourly, he cannot forgive himself. It seems the crazy darkness, having left her, or at least being en-route to a complete departure, is now returning to him. Sticky stuff, this dark-crazy epidemic.

Nothing anyone can do or say has succeeded in coaxing him from his little cell. The policemen, both of them, are getting tired of looking after him, and complain that if there were to be another criminal incident in the town, they'd have nowhere to put the culprit and one of them would have to take the felon home with them.

Also, now that he's been here a few days, he's beginning to smell. He won't wash, since he feels his sinner's body doesn't deserve purification, and he won't take his clothes off so they can wash them, because he says he must remain in them now till they turn to rags as an outward demonstration of his remorse and penitence for all the sins he has committed in his miserable life.

Miserable life indeed then, inside that stinky jailhouse.

Final recourse to his family, the ones he was visiting, failed to deliver results as he is still bearing a tiny grudge against them for not seeing things his way days ago, even though they were right and even he doesn't see things his old way now.

One last brain flicker suggests one last possible solution – they must see if the old woman is in a fit state to come to the jail and show him she is ok, and if she could put on a show of forgiveness ("might be asking a bit much", the policemen think) then they might finally get him to leave.

And so, in this their moment of despair at being driven out of their police station by the smell of unwashed sinner, the policemen, leaving the cell door ajar and the front door unlocked, to no effect of course, make their way up the hill to the little house of flowers, to make their appeal for liberation from their small personal hell.

* * *

Sitting around the veranda table, sipping cordial, polite comments are exchanged about how well she is looking, and how the crazy visitor clearly did no lasting harm, thank goodness, and leading questions are asked, though all see through them, about whether she has managed to walk into town yet, and has she seen any one of her neighbours since the incident.

It's a small town. Of course all have heard of the crazy visitor squatting in the only jail cell, even the dual mother in her sick bed, so when the policemen ramble coyly round and round the subject, fearful of getting to the point, she decides it's time to help them out.

"Ok, what do you want me to do?" she asks them. Flushing red at the ease with which their ruse has been flushed out, they mutter and mumble and talk over each other a bit, and finally come out with it – they'd like her to come to the jail, show him she's alive, and coax him out of there.

Uproar. The girls (minus the eldest whose head still throbs and has taken to her bed) roar their objections, crowding round their mother as if to physically prevent her moving any closer to that maniac who maimed her once and nearly caused her to vanish from them completely, and he's never going to be given the chance again. They're happy he's in jail and are happy for him to stay there permanently thank you very much, and they and their mother (speaking for her, clearly) want no part in helping him to freedom to maim again.

Hm. This isn't how the policemen saw this panning out. They are about to try another tactic when the old woman decides to speak for herself.

"Tell him I forgive him. Tell him he's still my friend in spite of all, and that he is invited here with his wife and children to see that I am well, and to celebrate our return to friendship."

"What?" demand the girls.

The old man looks at his wife in amazement, but since he made his own tour of penance around their old grey town, he has a better understanding of letting old grief and new grief and old and new anger and grudges and unhappiness, go, since he sees now what a burden they are to the person who carries them, so he not only understands but also applauds, silently, his wife's bold decision to invite her assailant into her home for tea.

The girls haven't made that big leap of understanding yet, and so battle with their mother's crazy-seeming decision, and wonder if the evil and loony new-her has briefly re-emerged. But she seems calm enough, and when she's her old self and has made a decision, they know a) not to question it too much and, b) that it is usually, ultimately, a good decision, so they keep quiet.

This, however, isn't the solution the policemen were hoping for. The problem is getting him out, so a solution that involves getting him to come out voluntarily seems like no solution at all, because he simply won't do it.

But they can't badger her. She's an invalid and a victim of crime, and not responsible for making their lives easier, so they finish their delicious cordials and rise, thanking her for her help, and promising to pass on the invitation.

They leave, heavier of heart than when they arrived, and trudge down the hill to their smelly workplace, pointlessly to pass on the worthless invitation to a man who will not entertain it.

Minutes after their return to their station, the crazy visitor emerges, blinks in the sunlight to which he has become unaccustomed during his days of incarceration, and heads for his transport and then for home.

As he passes the square he slows and glances up the hill towards the house, and his gaze lingers, a succession of emotions travelling across his features as his mind makes a journey back in time to when they were friends and all was normal and as it should be and should have remained throughout their lives.

He registers surprise at her invitation, and awe, and a promise of penance still, and anticipation at old friendships renewed and forgiveness for harm done, and moving on, from all the darkness of the past and the recent craziness. All will be well. All will be and is new, refreshed, starting over.

And so he trots slowly out of town and homewards to get his family and return with them to celebrate old times and new and future good times together.

That's all he wanted – his old friends back – but they had to see how cross he was first. Small thought, bigger actions, calm resolution, ultimately.

* * *

And so all is well again in the little town of hope and baking and friendships born and renewed and refreshed like they have been hosed down after a dust storm.

The girls, including the eldest who has come downstairs now the policemen have gone and the handsome one won't be able to eye her the way he does, which makes her nervous and annoyed and not at all jittery and giggly afterwards the way her sisters say it does. Ok, a little, but not the way they think. Well maybe a bit. Oh what do they know? They're just babies.

Anyway, all are chattering animatedly, anxious, rattled, excited, amazed that their life, which was so seamlessly dull and sad and uneventful for so many years, has become full of change and action and excitement, one new thing biting at the heels of another as they hurtle at high speed into this new phase in their new lives.

Returned father, returned mother, now soon to be returned old friends, best friends, all too much, and the youngest gets over excited and bursts into tears and has to be comforted by their returned mother, which overwhelms her and brings all the stress of the past few days to the surface, and she bawls for what seems like hours, till they think they're going to have to get the doctor for her too.

By evening though, all is calm once more and the moon and stars rise and glimmer over a tranquil scene. Girls in bed, reunited husband and wife, mother and father, in chairs pushed close together, holding hands in the scented darkness, their minds silently speaking vows and promises of love, honour, in sickness and health, for better or worse, and on into the universe of their hearts and souls that are now mingled, their energies and essences joined since that moment when he pressed his heart to hers and conjoined them finally, truly, for all time.

Blessed couple. Blessed family. Blessed house that contains so much love and forgiveness and renewal and rebirth, the cycle going on and on into infinity as they sleep and gaze in silent communion with each other and the universe.

And God is watching of course, smiling, satisfied. Job done. Good work. Another destiny achieved and made good, another batch of souls on track with their learning and experiencing which will make them better people, the girls better adults and wives and mothers and anchors in their community, to pass on the lessons hard-learnt and make the journeys of others a little easier by their experience.

Blessed journeys, blessed life, blessings to all. Amen.

THE END

Lightning Source UK Ltd.
Milton Keynes UK
171546UK00001B/56/P